"I have my patients to think of," Nora told him.

"I can't allow just anyone access to their information."

She was still fighting, even after the battle was lost. A part of Rob admired her tenacity. Yet while he admired her determination to get rid of him in spite of the pressure on her, Rob couldn't help but wonder why.

"Do you have something to hide, Dr. Blake?"

Her head snapped around and she stared at him with wide eyes. For a second, he thought he saw fear in their depths, but it was quickly replaced with anger. The elevator doors opened and she rushed off. He followed

than

Home

love deep in the heart

Books by Patricia Davids

Love Inspired

His Bundle of Love
Love Thine Enemy
Prodigal Daughter
The Color of Courage
Military Daddy
A Matter of the Heart

PATRICIA DAVIDS

Patricia Davids continues to work as a part-time nurse in the NICU while writing full-time. She enjoys researching new stories, traveling to new locations and meeting fans along the way. She and her husband live in Wichita, Kansas, along with the newest addition to the household, a stray cat named Spooky. Pat always enjoys hearing from her readers. You can contact her by mail at P.O. Box 16714 Wichita, Kansas 67216, or visit her on the Web at www.patriciadavids.com.

A Matter of the Heart
Patricia Davids

Steeple
Hill®

Published by Steeple Hill Books™

Special thanks and acknowledgment to
Patricia Davids for her contribution to the
Homecoming Heroes miniseries.

STEEPLE HILL BOOKS

Steeple
Hill®

ISBN-13: 978-0-373-81378-0
ISBN-10:   0-373-81378-3

A MATTER OF THE HEART

May he turn our hearts to him, to walk in all his ways and to keep the commands, decrees and regulations he gave our fathers.
—*1 Kings* 8:58

To Lenora Worth, Marta Perry, Brenda Coulter, Margaret Daley and Jillian Hart. Working with y'all has been a pleasure. Thanks for all the help you gave me.

Chapter One

"Excuse me, where is the patient I'm operating on this morning?" Dr. Nora Blake stood impatiently at the nurses' station in the Pediatric Intensive Care Unit. Two nurses in brightly colored uniforms were laughing about something until they heard her voice. Then they immediately fell silent, their smiles vanishing.

Nora knew she wasn't a favorite with the staff. She didn't possess the people skills many of her colleagues displayed. Her insistence on attention to detail and her intolerance of mediocre work had earned her the reputation of being difficult.

It wasn't that she didn't care what her coworkers thought of her—she did. It hurt to see how quickly their expressions changed from cheerful to guarded, but making sure her patients received the highest quality care was far more important than being popular.

Arching one eyebrow, the slender nurse with short blond hair asked, "Do you mean Cara Dempsey?"

Nora raised her chin. Her skill was saving children with heart defects, not winning popularity contests. Professionalism was the key to getting things done right in the hospital, not sociability.

"I'm looking for the patient who came in from Blackwater General yesterday with transposition of the great arteries. Do you have the chart?" The words came out sounding sharper than she intended.

The ward nurse held out a black three-ring binder. "The patient is in room five. Dr. Kent just finished talking to the parents."

"Thank you." Nora nodded, relieved to hear that her partner had arrived first. Peter Kent would have explained the coming procedure to the family. It saved Nora the time and headache of trying to make laypeople understand the complex nature of the upcoming operation.

If she found any fault with Peter, who was ten years her senior and had been her partner for the past two years, it was that he was too upbeat in dealing with the families. As far as she was concerned, he often sugarcoated the truth and offered false hope. She would need to impress on the Dempsey family the risks involved, especially for an infant. Not every patient survived open-heart surgery.

Thumbing through the chart, she paid special attention to the laboratory values and medications being given to the two-day-old infant. Satisfied that everything had been done correctly, she closed the binder and moved to the computer in the corner of the desk area reserved for use by physicians. She pulled up the echocardiogram images of her patient.

She had already studied the scans extensively in her office late last night, but she wanted to make sure that she hadn't missed anything, so she watched the movie of the child's beating heart one more time. As always, a profound sense of wonder and awe engulfed her. The human heart was a beautiful thing.

She quickly focused on gathering the information she would need to repair the child's flawed heart. Operating on a newborn baby was always hard for her. It brought back too many painful memories. She preferred her patients to be at least six months old, but this child wouldn't live a week without surgery. It had to be done now.

The quality of the echocardiogram and tests were excellent, but Nora wouldn't know what she was actually dealing with until she looked inside the patient's chest. If there was one thing that she had learned during her years of training, it was that every heart was unique.

Leaving the desk, Nora walked to room five. Outside, she paused a moment to brace herself. Drawing a deep breath, she pasted a smile on her face, knocked once and then entered.

Inside, she saw a young couple sitting on the small couch at the back of the room with their arms around each other for support. They both had red-rimmed eyes, either from crying or from lack of sleep or both. They looked shell-shocked and barely out of their teens—far too young to be facing what lay ahead.

They both rose to their feet, and their hopeful eyes begged her for help she wasn't sure she could give. For a split second she envied them each having someone to hold on to during the coming hours. She had been in their shoes once with no one to comfort her. The memory of those terrible days haunted her still.

On the warming bed, a baby girl with thick dark hair lay unnaturally still. A white tube taped to her mouth connected her to a ventilator. IV pumps and monitors took up most of the space around her and beeped softly. Drugs kept her from moving and fighting the very machines that were keeping her alive. Even with the ventilator breathing for her, the child's lips were dark blue. It wasn't a good sign.

Nora nodded at the parents. "I'm Dr. Blake and I'll be performing your child's surgery this morning."

The father spoke quickly. "You can make her well, can't you? Doctor Kent, he said you were the best."

"As you know, your daughter was born with the blood vessels leading from the heart in the wrong places. Outcomes are usually good with this procedure, but five percent of the children who have this done don't survive or survive with serious brain damage. You need to be aware of that."

Cara's mother laid a loving hand on her daughter's small head. "God will be with you and with Cara. He will save her. God can do anything."

Nora bit back the comment that rose to her lips. She didn't share this young mother's belief in a benevolent God, but she had learned that revealing her philosophy with families frequently increased their anxiety.

Instead, she said, "I'll meet with you in the

surgical waiting room when the operation is over. It will take several hours, but one of the staff will come out to give you updates during that time."

The door to the room opened and the blond nurse looked in. "Mr. and Mrs. Dempsey, would you please step out to the desk? I have some forms for you to sign."

As the couple followed the nurse out into the hall, Nora found herself alone with her patient. Looking down at the baby depending on her for so much, she experienced a pang of overwhelming compassion. Reaching out, she stroked the child's hair with one hand. The tiny curls were soft as silk.

"If God can do anything, then why am I always fixing His mistakes?" Nora whispered.

She touched the small oval locket that hung on a gold chain around her neck. There was no answer to her question today. There never had been.

Catching her lower lip between her teeth, she closed her eyes and regained the composure she would need in surgery. Intense focus, not sympathy, would save this child.

After leaving the baby's room, Nora headed to the elevators. At the fifth floor, she stepped out and walked quickly toward the operating suites.

She passed the pre-op nurses' station without pausing, barely noticing the women in green surgical garbs identical to her own standing in a group behind the tall, black granite counter.

Her mind was already intent on the delicate surgery she would be doing in the next few minutes. She rehearsed each move in detail.

Step-by-step, she visualized the course of the entire procedure, taking into account the obstacles and challenges the walnut-sized heart of this baby might present. Once the operation was under way, timing would be critical. The child couldn't afford to have her surgeon wondering what to do next.

The hallway led her past the family waiting room outside the surgery doors. Nora didn't bother glancing in. The parents would stay upstairs until the OR and PICU staff moved the baby to the surgery. If all went well, Nora would find Mr. and Mrs. Dempsey in about four hours and tell them their baby was still alive.

If all went well? It was a big if. There were so many things that could go wrong.

"Dr. Blake, may I have a word with you, please?"

Startled by the sound of a deep male voice behind her, Nora spun around. It took her a second to place the tall man with wavy dark brown hair who stepped out of the waiting room. When she did, she scowled.

Mr. Robert Dale, persistent reporter for the *Liberty and Justice* newspaper jogged toward her.

He was a man most women would notice. Dressed in jeans and a blue button-down shirt, he exuded confidence. His long stride and easy grace had her guessing that he was a runner, an activity that she enjoyed as often as her work permitted. His rugged features and deep tan made it clear that he preferred the outdoors over a treadmill. His bright blue eyes were fixed on her now with the intensity of a sprinter sighting the finish line.

She didn't intend to become his journalistic prize.

"I'm on my way to surgery, Mr. Dale. I'm afraid I don't have time to answer your questions."

Not bothering to hide her annoyance, she turned back toward the OR and quickened her pace. The wide, gray metal doors were only a few yards away. He couldn't follow her in there.

The man had been practically stalking her in his quest for information about the Ali Tabiz Willis case. The story of a five-year-old war orphan from the Middle East being flown to Texas for life-saving open-heart surgery apparently made a good human interest story. At least, Mr. Dale's paper seemed to think it did.

Or maybe they were so interested because the boy's grandfather was a retired U.S. Army general.

Either way, Mr. Dale had called her office enough times over the past few days that she had finally instructed her secretary to stop taking his messages. It seemed he couldn't take a hint.

A sudden thought struck her—how had he found out that she would be here? She hadn't known until late last night that she would be doing surgery this morning. Annoyance flared into anger at the possibility that her secretary or one of the hospital nurses had informed him of her schedule.

Determined to find out who had leaked the information, she spun around to confront him. Her abrupt change in direction caught him off guard and he plowed into her. The impact knocked her backward.

His strong hands shot out and grabbed her arms to keep her upright. "Sorry about that, Doc."

The feel of his long fingers curled around her

bare arms triggered a thrill of awareness that shocked her. She drew a deep breath to steady her nerves. It didn't help. Instead, it flooded her senses with the masculine scent of his after-shave and a hint of caramel coffee.

She focused her gaze on a small damp stain on his pale blue shirt. He must have sloshed coffee on himself just as she walked by the waiting room. The thought that he had been lurking there expressly to waylay her brought her anger rushing back. She used it to suppress the strange and unbidden attraction she felt as she jerked away from him. "Who told you I'd be here this morning?"

His eyes sparkled with mirth and a grin tugged at the corner of his mouth, revealing a dimple in one cheek. For a split second, she envied his self-confidence and friendly poise.

"Now, Doc, you know a reporter never reveals his sources. Besides, you haven't returned my calls. I wasn't left with much choice except to track you down at work."

She rubbed her upper arms trying to dispel the tingle his touch caused. "How often do you have to hear that I have no comment, Mr. Dale?"

"Call me Rob."

"I prefer not to, Mr. Dale." She turned and began walking away.

He quickly fell into step beside her. "I'd like to know why you object so strongly to being interviewed about Ali Willis's case?"

"Medical information is privileged. I'm sure you are already aware of that."

"I have copies of a release from the boy's guardian as well as from the Children of the Day organization. Would you like to see them?" He pulled several folded sheets of paper from his hip pocket.

Ignoring the missives, she paused long enough to swipe her ID badge in front of a small black sensor on the wall. The OR doors swung open, revealing a flurry of activity as men and women dressed in green scrubs moved patients on gurneys and carts loaded with supplies and equipment through the wide, brightly lit halls.

She paused to glare at the man following her with a small sense of triumph. "I won't help your paper or anyone else profit from a child's suffering. We're done. You aren't allowed in here. If you don't leave, I'll have security remove you."

Granting Rob Dale or any reporter an interview was the last thing she wanted to do. It was their job to pry, to uncover stories and reveal secrets. There were things in her past that were best left undisturbed.

He stepped back as the doors began to close but leaned to the side to keep eye contact with her. "If you won't talk to me about Ali, why don't we talk about the Children of the Day organization? I'll buy you a cup of coffee."

She merely arched one eyebrow and waited until the steel panels clicked shut, eliminating him from her sight.

The man was certainly persistent…and attractive. There was no denying that fact. Not once since her husband's death six years ago had a man affected her so strongly. Her reaction to the reporter was an aberration, but not something she couldn't handle. Rob Dale would have to take no for an answer this time and she wouldn't have to deal with him again.

Closing her eyes, she reached up and curled her fingers tenderly around the locket at her neck. She had more important things to think about than a man with friendly blue eyes, an engaging grin and strong hands that sent shivers down her spine when he touched her.

This is crazy. Get him out of your head. Refocus.

Forcing thoughts of the man out of her mind, she tucked the locket beneath the scooped neck of her top and proceeded into the scrub room. A long morning loomed ahead of her.

* * *

Rob admitted only temporary defeat as the doors closed between him and the intriguing doctor with shoulder-length blond hair, a cute upturned nose and intense hazel eyes. Dr. Blake might not want to speak to him, but he wasn't about to give up so easily. His paper had sent him to do a story. It wasn't an earth-shattering feature, but he would have to make do until a better story came his way.

He returned to the waiting room and scooped up his interrupted cup of mocha caramel latte. After taking a sip, he walked back down the hallway. Perhaps he could get what he needed for the story without using Dr. Blake.

At the nurses' station, he paused to speak to the short, friendly brunette who had told him of Dr. Blake's surgical schedule after only the mildest probing earlier that morning.

"You were right," he said, leaning both elbows on the waist-high countertop and gracing her with his best smile.

She closed the chart she was writing on and stuck it in a silver wire rack. "I told you Dr. Ice Princess wouldn't give you the time of day."

An older nurse seated beside her looked up and said, "Traci, that's no way to talk about Dr. Blake. She's an excellent surgeon. Your patient has just arrived in pre-op number two. I think you're needed there."

Traci rolled her eyes and rose with an exaggerated sigh. "I didn't invent the title, Emily, and you know she's earned it."

Rob watched her walk away, then turned his attention and his smile on the woman still seated at a long desk behind the counter. "Emily, it's nice to meet you. I'm Rob Dale. I'm doing a story on a little boy having surgery soon named Ali Willis."

"We aren't allowed to give out patient information."

"Of course, and I wouldn't ask you to do that. I already know that Dr. Blake will be doing the surgery, and I'm interested in finding out more about *her*. I've been told she does quite a bit of charity work. That doesn't sound like an ice princess to me."

Emily sent a wary look his way, but he gave her his most disarming grin.

After a moment, she relaxed and said, "If she does, she doesn't advertise the fact, but then I've never known her to give an interview. She's a very private person."

Or she has something to hide, he mused to himself. In the past he'd often found that the people who didn't want to talk to him were the ones that deserved a closer look. The phone on the desk rang, and Emily excused herself to answer it.

Rob straightened but he didn't move away. With half an ear, he listened in on Emily's end of the conversation. Dr. Blake's reluctance to talk to him had piqued his interest. The fact that she was prettier than any surgeon he'd ever met made him consider trying to interview her again, but his assignment was to do an in-depth piece on Children of the Day, a Christian charity devoted to helping innocent victims of war, not specifically on Dr. Blake. The only reason he was here was because of her work for the organization.

It was a fluff piece, but while he was in the States, he had to go where he was assigned. He glanced down at the red puckered scar on his forearm and flexed the fingers of his left hand. He was as healed as he was going to get. How many more of these feel-good stories would he have to do before he could return to the real action?

"You're not staying home from school unless you're running a fever, young man. Let me talk to your father."

Rob couldn't help but smile at Emily's un-sympathetic tone. He and his three brothers had been subjected to the same stern speech plenty of times while they were growing up. How did mothers everywhere know when their kids were faking it? However they did it, it would be a useful trait for a reporter to learn.

Rob's cell phone began to ring. A surge of anticipation shot through him when he recognized the distinctive tone he had set for his boss and friend, Derrick Mitchell, the senior editor of *Liberty and Justice*.

Maybe I'm getting reassigned at last. Please, Lord, let it be the Middle East post that's open.

Rob walked a few steps away from the desk and answered on the third ring.

"Rob, where are you on the Willis story?" Derrick's voice crackled with impatience.

"Hello to you, too, Derrick. I'm still in Austin trying to get an interview with the boy's surgeon, but she's not talking."

An orderly pushing a gurney came down the hall. Stepping aside to let the bed transporting an elderly man pass by, Rob frowned at the silence on the other end of his connection. Maybe Derrick was worried about Rob making the deadline.

Quickly, Rob said, "I don't think she's that important to the piece. I know you said I had until the end of October to get the story in, but I can have the rest of it on your desk in two weeks. A week if you need to rush it. Then I'll be free to take the Middle East assignment that's open. It's my old stomping grounds. With the people I know in the area, I'll be a real asset to the paper there."

Stateside reporting was okay, but nothing was as thrilling as reporting from inside a war zone. He missed it—a lot.

"I'm sorry, Rob. I know how much you want that post, but I'm sending Dick Carter."

Pressing a hand to his forehead in disbelief, Rob said, "You're joking, right? Carter's a greenhorn."

"He's got a nose for a story and he's done some great work for us. You'll want to check out his piece on the baggage handlers at Memdelholm Airfield."

"Memdelholm was my piece."

"Your piece about their special handling of packages to deployed servicemen was good— touching even. Carter's piece about their drug-smuggling ring using phony names and addresses of Americans overseas is dynamite. It's on today's front page."

"What? That's crazy. I know men in charge there. Drake Manns and Benny Chase are both buddies of mine. They wouldn't be involved in something illegal."

"I'm afraid your friends are involved up to their necks. They were both arrested a few hours ago. My sources say they've pled guilty and are each trying to cut a deal."

Thankful that there was a solid wall behind him, Rob leaned back and covered his eyes with his hand. "I can't believe it. I served with Drake and Benny for three years. Benny saved my life. They're great guys. They have so much respect for the men still serving."

"Didn't you have an inkling that things weren't right?"

"They were reluctant to talk about their work, but I thought it was humility. Drake said they didn't want me singing their praises. I trusted them."

Rob couldn't believe how much it hurt knowing someone he had served with had deceived him. How could he have been so easily mislead? That a raw newcomer like Carter had uncovered the story stung even more. "Oh, man. I really blew it, didn't I?"

"You're a good reporter, Dale. People open up to you. You could charm the U.S. Mint out of its gold and my grandmother out of her secret mincemeat pie recipe, but your trouble is that you prefer to see the good in people. You didn't dig deep enough."

"Overseas it was so black and white. We were the good guys, they were the bad guys."

"That's your army mentality speaking. You aren't a soldier anymore. Your obligation is to report all sides of a story, even when it casts some of our servicemen or women in a poor light. The truth needs to be told, even when it hurts. That's what journalism is."

Looking down, Rob shoved his free hand into his front jean pocket. "Am I fired?"

"I've given Carter a monthlong trial assignment in our Middle East bureau. If he does well, I may make it permanent. I haven't decided yet."

"Then there's a chance I can go back?"

"All I'm going to say is dig deeper, Rob. Make every story important. Use your instincts. Don't make me regret giving you this job."

Derrick hung up, and after a second Rob closed his own phone. He stuffed it in his front pocket but didn't move from his place outside the surgical waiting room.

How could he have missed that his buddies at Memdelholm were involved in something shady? The fact that he had been so easily deceived was hard to swallow.

Derrick's right. I wasn't looking hard enough. I thought it was a simple piece and I blew it.

When he had been among the soldiers and

marines on the front lines, the best stories had all but fallen into his lap. Over there, his gut instincts were never wrong. He knew that world inside and out.

He needed to be back there, but that wasn't going to happen now. Not until he proved to Derrick Mitchell that he had what it took to get to the bottom of any story.

Lord, I failed to make the most of Your gift. It won't happen again. You sent me here for a reason. I don't know what that reason is, but I'm going to keep looking until I find it.

He glanced toward the surgery doors. His gut told him that Dr. Nora Blake was more than a woman who didn't grant interviews. He had no idea what a woman like her might be hiding, but he was going to find out. He intended to dig deep.

Chapter Two

"You can't be serious!"

In stunned disbelief, Nora sat in the black leather chair in front of Willard Branson, the CEO and chief administrator of Mercy Medical Center, and stared openmouthed at her boss. In the chair beside hers, Rob Dale sat with a smile on his face that wasn't quite a self-satisfied smirk, but it was close.

She had hoped that their confrontation outside of surgery the day before yesterday would have convinced the reporter to leave her alone. Apparently, it hadn't.

His audacity provoked a slow burn of irritation, but it didn't prevent her from noticing how attractive he looked in charcoal slacks, a sage dress shirt that accentuated his lean, athletic body and a tasteful silk tie that made her wonder if a wife or girlfriend had picked it out for him.

"I'm perfectly serious, Dr. Blake," Willard replied, drawing her attention back to him. "You are free to donate as much time and energy as you wish to Children of the Day, and I applaud your dedication to the organization, but the hospital must weigh the pros and cons of each case. We have already donated many hours of the staff's time and much of our limited resources to helping your cause. It's time we got something back."

"Saving the lives of needy children isn't enough payback for you?" She didn't bother hiding her sarcasm.

Steepling his fingers together, Willard leaned forward on his wide mahogany desk. "I hired you because you had a reputation for being the brightest new pediatric cardiologist to come out of the Cleveland Clinic in years. I hired you because I wanted someone who could grow our program."

"Haven't I done that?"

"You have to an extent. Your surgical success rate is impressive, but the publicity generated by a series of articles like Mr. Dale is proposing could very well increase the number of patients referred to this facility. Patients you will operate on.

"It might even generate substantial donations to us and to Children of the Day. I'm sure I don't need to remind you that *Liberty and Justice* is an international and very well-respected paper. Frankly, I don't understand why you aren't jumping at this opportunity."

Everything Willard said was true, but Nora couldn't abide the thought of someone poking about in her life and in her work.

She tried one last avenue. "I'm sure Dr. Kent would be delighted to have Mr. Dale shadow him on a day-to-day basis."

"But he doesn't do volunteer work for Children of the Day," Rob interjected.

She glared at him. "Dr. Kent has aided me a number of times. If you're so interested in the organization, I suggest you spend your time with Anna Terenkov. She is the founder of Children of the Day. I'm certain she will answer any questions you have."

"I've already spoken to Ms. Terenkov. She's the one who pointed out how frequently your expertise has been utilized even before little Ali Willis's case was brought to their attention."

He pulled a small notebook from his shirt pocket, flipped it open and began to read. "And I quote, 'Dr. Blake is personally responsible for saving the lives of a dozen children in the past year who would otherwise have died of their congenital heart defects in war-torn third world countries.

"'Besides doing these surgeries without compensation, she has been instrumental in convincing Mercy Medical Center to provide the additional care needed at a greatly reduced fee. She oversees the donated medical supplies and has convinced numerous drug companies to donate badly needed medications—medicines that families in these countries would otherwise have to buy on the black market at exorbitant prices.'"

He paused and looked up. "Shall I continue? There's a lot more. Like the fact that you also work part-time at Fort Bonnell Medical Center and have even traveled overseas on a medical mission for Children of the Day. It must be difficult to maintain any kind of private life with this much on your plate."

"I'm well aware of my workload, and my private life is off-limits. Is that understood?"

His eyes brightened. "Then you'll allow me to tag along with you for Ali's surgery?"

She glanced at Willard, the man responsible for hiring her and approving the amount of charity work Mercy did. He nodded slightly.

She closed her eyes in resignation. "It seems I have little choice."

"You won't regret it, I promise," Rob quickly assured her.

"Strange, but I already do." She looked at Willard. "Are we done here? I have rounds to make."

She hated confrontations, especially when she didn't emerge the winner.

"We're done, Dr. Blake. Mr. Dale, when would you like to start?"

"There's no time like the present. Care to show me around, Dr. Blake? May I call you Nora?"

She rose to her feet already uncomfortable with his close scrutiny. How was she going to tolerate having him around for days? She had to see that he kept his distance. Cool professionalism was the key.

"You may address me as Dr. Blake. Ali's surgery isn't scheduled for another two weeks. I see no reason for you to hound me until then."

He tucked his pad and pen back in his shirt pocket. "I'll need some background information about how heart surgery is carried out, and the best way would be for me to see a few surgeries for myself."

"I'm not taking you into the operating room."

Turning on her heel, Nora left the CEO's office

and walked quickly toward the elevators. She knew Rob was following without looking back.

"Now, Nora, I know that you have students and visiting physicians who observe your surgeries. It won't be any different having me in the room."

For some reason, she knew it would. She was aware of him on a level that she had never experienced before. The last thing she wanted was him disturbing her concentration while she was operating.

At the end of the hall, she punched the down arrow and the elevator doors immediately slid open. The car was empty. Why couldn't it have been crowded? She stepped inside and turned to face the opening. Rob slipped in behind her. The doors closed, shutting them in together.

Music played softly overhead. She could see a blurred reflection of herself and Rob in the brightly polished metal panels. The simple white blouse and fitted navy skirt that she had picked out that morning made her look like a schoolgirl instead of a thirty-five-year-old woman with a demanding career.

The scent of his cologne tickled her nose. It was a brand she liked, and on him it smelled particularly good—spicy but not overpowering. She tried not to breath.

His reflection leaned toward hers. She tensed as he spoke; his breath tickled her earlobe and the nape of her neck. "I think you have to push the button."

Blood rushed to her face, staining it crimson above her white collar. She jabbed her finger into the button for the third floor so hard it hurt.

Rob leaned away from Nora and let his gaze skim over her trim figure. She was tall for a woman, maybe five foot eight or five foot nine. She wore her hair pulled back into a French twist today, and the style accentuated the graceful curve of her neck. She radiated cool grace.

"I have my patients to think of, Mr. Dale. I can't allow just anyone access to their information."

She was still fighting even after the battle was lost. A part of him admired her tenacity.

"Mr. Branson has made me aware of the patient confidentiality issues. Everything I see or hear regarding patients will remain strictly confidential."

While he might admire her determination to get rid of him in spite of the pressure Willard Branson put on her, Rob couldn't help but wonder why. He decided to try a direct approach.

"Do you have something to hide, Dr. Blake?"

Her head snapped around and she stared at him with wide eyes. For a second, he thought he saw fear in their depths, but it was quickly replaced by anger. She turned her back on him. "I have no idea why you would even suggest such a thing."

The elevator doors opened and she rushed off. He followed at a slower pace, but more intrigued than ever. She entered the second doorway on the left and slammed it shut behind her.

After pausing to read her name and the name of her partner stenciled in gold lettering on the glass panel, he made a mental note to look up her partner's credentials. Rob had already checked Nora's. They were impressive.

He opened the door and stuck his head inside. A middle-aged woman with impossibly black hair teased in a 1970s flip sat behind an immaculate rosewood desk centered between two identical doors. Nora stood beside her. Two additional open doorways at each end of the reception area revealed examination rooms that were currently empty.

Rob winked at the secretary. "You must be Carmen. I'm Rob Dale. Is it safe to come in?"

She hid a smile with difficulty as she glanced between Nora and him. "For the moment."

"Good." He entered the stark office with plain white walls and a half dozen reception-style maroon chairs lining the perimeter. "How's Harold getting along?"

"He's much better, thank you."

Nora's frown deepened as she glared at her secretary. "Do you know this man?"

Rob walked forward and grasped Carmen's plump fingers. He gave them a squeeze. "We've spoken on the phone so many times this week that I feel like Carmen is an old friend."

Carmen batted her eyes. "You're just as charming in person as you are on the telephone."

"Not nearly as charming as you are. I would have braved the dragon days ago if I had known how pretty you were. I'm so glad to hear Harold is doing better. I've been praying for him."

Nora's mouth dropped open. "Who are you calling a dragon and who is Harold?"

"Harold is Carmen's husband. He had a nasty bout of pneumonia. It's a good thing her daughter was able to come over and take care of him since Carmen couldn't get time off from work," Rob said, enjoying Nora's obvious confusion.

Nora folded her arms across her chest as she frowned at her secretary. "You didn't mention you needed time off."

Tilting her head to one side, Carmen said,

"Actually, I did ask for a few days off last week, but you said your schedule was full and that I was needed here."

"Oh, yes. I remember that. Well…you should have made a point of telling me it was a family emergency."

"I'll be more clear in the future, Dr. Blake."

"Carmen is not my regular secretary," Nora said, giving Rob a pointed look.

Carmen nodded. "I'm a temp. I fill in for Delia when she takes time off. She goes to Vegas every chance she gets. I think she has a boyfriend there."

"All right then." Nora's smile looked forced. "Carmen, Mr. Dale will be shadowing me for a few days. Please get him a set of scrubs."

Rising from her chair, Carmen said, "Dr. Kent has several sets in his office. I'll get one for you. You look about the same size."

Nora walked toward the inner office on the right and Rob followed.

Inside, a quick glance around the room revealed a large oak desk with two chairs facing it. They matched the chairs lining the outer office—none of which looked made for comfort. On the desk were an oversized paper pad and a computer screen. Several filing cabinets sat beneath a wide window with a nice view of downtown Austin in the distance. A tall, gray metal wardrobe took up the remaining space in the corner. There was a closed door on the near wall. Rob assumed it connected to the exam room. On the opposite wall was a small taupe sofa. He crossed the room and sat down.

Reaching out, he plucked several long blond hairs from a faint depression in the padded arm. A green-and-red plaid throw blanket lay draped over the other end of the couch.

"Do you sleep here a lot?" he asked, looking to where she stood pulling open the small wardrobe.

She withdrew a set of green scrubs on hangers. "Occasionally, when I need to remain in the hospital."

"Your home is in Prairie Springs, isn't it? That's only thirty minutes from here."

"Thirty minutes is a long time when a patient needs their chest reopened." Spinning around, she held the scrubs close to her chest like a flimsy cloth shield. "How do you know where I live?"

He rose from the sofa and crossed to stand in front of the wall behind her desk where a half dozen framed certificates hung in two neat rows.

"I do my research, Nora. You graduated from Albertville High School in Boston at the precocious age of fifteen and at the head of your class. You finished pre-med at Columbia in three years and entered medical school with top honors. You joined the army and studied at Walter Reed where you chose to specialize in cardiac surgery. After that, you did your peds cardiac fellowship at the Cleveland Clinic. You were married briefly—"

"I know my own history," she interrupted quickly.

"Of course."

He turned to study the silver-framed photo on her desk. Picking it up, he compared the young woman's face in the picture to Nora's. There wasn't a resemblance. The snapshot was of a smiling woman in her early twenties with thick brown hair that cascaded around a delicate oval face. "Pretty girl. Who is she?"

Nora took the frame from him and replaced it in the exact spot at the right-hand corner of her desk. "My stepdaughter. Since you seem to be so well versed about me, Mr. Dale, I think it's only fair that you reciprocate."

He held his hands wide. "My life is an open book."

"Somehow, I doubt that."

"What would you like to know? I graduated from high school in Dodge City, Kansas—not even close to the top of my very small class. I drifted between majors at the local junior college and finally ended up in the army. It didn't take me long to realize that I wanted to be a ranger. Those guys do the fun stuff. Twelve years later, I decided I was getting too old to go jumping out of planes. A desk job or training new recruits didn't appeal to me, so I opted to leave the service."

"How does one decide that digging into other people's lives makes a worthwhile second profession?"

"That was easy. I was sitting in a café in the busy capital of a small Middle Eastern country and relating the tale of how I met a pair of gun-runners to some friends. A man at the next table leaned over and asked me if I could help him get an interview with the unsavory duo. The guy turned out to be Derrick Mitchell, a senior reporter for *Liberty and Justice*. When my story panned out, he got promoted and asked me to come to work for him."

"Just like that? You didn't study journalism for years or work your way up from copy boy to the newsroom?"

Her sarcasm didn't offend him. He rather enjoyed the way she lifted her chin and tried to talk down to him although she was a good four inches shorter than his six-foot frame. He sensed it was a ruse designed to put him off. It didn't work.

"Nope. The job just fell into my lap. I believe the good Lord puts me where I am needed most."

She looked down and smoothed the fabric she held with one hand. "Yes, I imagine you would have a simplistic outlook. I think a person should have to work hard to achieve what they want, otherwise it is meaningless."

"You don't believe that God led you to become a surgeon in Austin?"

She gave an emphatic shake of her head. "No. It took fifteen years of hard study, grueling clinical hours and painstaking attention to detail. I've earned my place here—it didn't fall into my lap. God had nothing to do with it."

Something about her answer intrigued him. At first he couldn't quite put his finger on what it was, then he knew. Her vehement denial of God's role in her life, like her sarcasm, didn't ring true. There was more to this woman than she allowed others to see. His sudden intense urge to understand her better caught him off guard.

This was more than his usual need to find the story behind the person. He studied her face for a long moment, noticing her high cheekbones and full lips, the stubborn jut of her chin and the delicate winged brows above her expressive eyes. And then it hit him.

He expected annoyance, even arrogance from her, but what he saw in Nora's eyes was infinite sadness—a longing for something precious that had been lost. In the war-torn countries where he had served he'd seen the same look all too often. It touched something deep inside him.

Gently, he said, "That doesn't mean God didn't lead you here. What made you stop believing?"

He watched the struggle on her face. For a second, it seemed as if he had connected with her, but the outer door opened and Carmen entered with a pair of scrubs over her arm.

The moment was lost and Nora turned away. Rob moved to take the scrubs from Carmen and offered his thanks. She nodded and left without speaking.

Nora closed the door of her closet. "I don't have time to argue the existence of a higher power with you, Mr. Dale. I have rounds to make. If you'll excuse me, I need to change. You may use the exam room through that door."

Her cool tone conveyed in more than words that she was done talking to him. Rob touched one finger to his forehead in a brief salute and pulled open the door she indicated. As it closed behind him, he heard the lock click with a snap. Unbuttoning his shirt, he acknowledged that he'd uncovered more questions than answers in his brief time with Dr. Nora Blake.

He looked forward to the rest of the day with a growing sense of anticipation that he hadn't experienced since he'd arrived back in the States. Dr. Nora Blake presented an intriguing puzzle—one he found himself eager to solve.

Nora walked to her chair and sank onto the familiar seat. A second later, she put her elbows on the desk and dropped her head into her hands.

Why now? Why after all these years? The pain of her past never truly went away, but there were days that she didn't think about those difficult, sad hours and what she had lost. In the past year, there had even been times when she didn't think about Bernard and the terrible debt she had to repay.

How ironic that the charity work she was doing to make amends was the very thing that might shine a spotlight on things best left hidden.

Looking up, she focused on Pamela's picture. Her stepdaughter had endured enough pain in her life. Nora wasn't about to let Rob Dale add to that burden.

He might appear cute and harmless, but so

did a terrier puppy. It was only after one had turned your backyard into a crater-filled moonscape that you realized their true purpose. They had been bred to dig out vermin.

Rob Dale of *Liberty and Justice* struck her as the same kind of animal. He was no one's lapdog.

She needed to steer him away from anything that involved her personal life. As a plan it wasn't much, but it was all she had.

She rose and quickly changed out of her skirt and blouse and into her scrubs. She didn't have any surgeries today, but she needed to follow up on three of her patients who were still in the hospital.

At the door leading out to the reception area, she paused with her hand on the knob. Letting Rob or anyone on the staff see her rattled would only undermine what she hoped to accomplish at Mercy Medical Center. When she felt she had control of her emotions, she exited the room with brisk strides. Rob, already changed, hastened to follow her.

"Where are we going?" he asked, working to tighten the drawstring on his scrub pants while he tried to keep pace with her.

"We are going to the PICU. That stands for Pediatric Intensive Care Unit. I have three patients there."

"I thought we were going to surgery."

"Not today, but I have an AV canal repair scheduled for the day after tomorrow."

"AV canal. What kind of injury is that?" He finished cinching up his pants and pulled a small notebook from his breast pocket.

"An atrial ventricular canal is a congenital cardiac defect, as are the vast majority of the patients I see at this hospital. When I work at the base hospital, I do mostly follow-ups on adult patients after bypass surgery."

They passed the elevators, but she didn't stop. Instead, she pushed open the stairwell door and headed up. Two floors later she opened another door and strode out onto the pediatric floor. Unlike the rest of the hospital, the walls here were brightly colored and decorated with oversized cutouts of cartoon characters.

Rob noticed she didn't seem winded by the rapid climb. "So you don't get many injures like Ali's?"

"To be perfectly honest, I have never seen a case like Ali's and I've only read about a very few in the literature. Most of them were adults involved in motor vehicle accidents. The vast majority of people who sustain enough trauma to tear apart an internal structure of the heart don't survive.

"The fact that Ali has is amazing. Two of the cases I studied healed on their own. Two required surgery to repair the tear when they began to show signs of fluid buildup in the lung. Three others died due to heart tissue death after approximately four days. However, Ali's operation will be the same as for a simple VSD repair."

"How can you operate on the kid if you haven't had a case like this before? What's a VSD?"

Nora paused outside a pair of wide double doors marked with PICU in large letters. "A VSD is a congenital cardiac defect."

"You said that before."

"And my answer was correct both times. We have several good handouts that we give to parents explaining the defects in detail and how they are repaired. I'll make sure Carmen gets you some to study."

"When do you see patients in your office?"

"Consults and a few follow-ups are scheduled once a week on Mondays. Ninety-five percent of my patients are direct admits to the PICU. Heart defects in children often go undetected until they are in crisis. Unless they have need of a second surgery in the future, I don't normally see them after they leave the hospital."

"Doesn't that make it hard to get to know the families?"

"My focus is on my patients, not the families. There are social workers and others who deal with any issues that arise with them."

Pushing open the doors, Nora entered the unit and walked to the nursing desk. Theresa Mabley, a stout woman with short salt-and-pepper hair was dressed in her usual blue scrubs. Standing behind her were a collection of residents and nurses, all waiting to begin reporting to Nora on the patients.

"Good morning, Theresa. Mr. Dale, this is the head nurse in our PICU. Mr. Dale is a reporter, and he'll be rounding with me for the next several days. You may answer any questions he has."

Theresa nodded in his direction. "Nice to meet you, Mr. Dale."

He extended his hand. "Call me Rob. I promise not to get underfoot more than fifty times a day, Theresa."

His lopsided grin gave him the look of a charming rogue, and it was painfully clear to Nora that even the stalwart charge nurse wasn't immune as Theresa shook his hand and smiled back at him. "I doubt you'll be underfoot at all, Rob. Is this your first visit to a PICU?"

"My very first. Be kind to me."

Theresa chuckled. "Let me give you the tour. We currently have an eight-bed unit. However, thanks to a recent quarter-million-dollar gift made to the hospital in our name, we'll soon be resuming construction to expand to a fifteen-bed unit with all new, state-of-the-art equipment."

Nora held her breath thinking he would ask questions about the money, but Theresa was already on to her favorite topics—the need for more nurses and her grandchildren.

Nora stared at the two of them. How did he do it? How did he connect with people so easily? She didn't get it. It had taken months for Theresa to warm up to Nora, and even now they were far from friends. Yet Theresa was chatting away with this reporter like she had known him for ages.

Suddenly, the code-blue alarm rang. Glancing down the hallway, she saw the light flashing over Cara Dempsey's doorway. Rob Dale was completely forgotten as Nora raced toward the room.

Chapter Three

Rob watched Nora bolt down the hallway. Several people in lab coats came running into the unit and rushed passed him, closely followed by a security officer. Rob had no idea what was going on, but it didn't look good.

He moved to where he could look through the door and yet be out of the way. All he could see was a ring of people crowding around a warming bed. Theresa entered the room, but she didn't join the crowd. Instead, she went to stand beside a young couple huddled together watching the activity with wide frightened eyes.

Draping an arm around the young woman's shoulder, the nurse gently explained to them what was going on. Rob couldn't hear everything over the noise of the alarms, but it was clear that their baby was in serious trouble.

The young mother burst into tears and pressed her hands to her mouth, then shouted, "Don't let her die! Please, God, I'll do anything, just don't let her die!"

Nora, at the side of the bed, looked up and motioned with her head toward the door. "Take them out of here, and someone silence that alarm!"

Theresa gently but firmly herded the couple out of the room. A tall, thin, young man with blond hair and dressed in a dark suit met them at the unit door and led them away. Rob noticed he was holding a Bible in one hand.

Theresa came back and stopped beside Rob. In a weary voice, she said, "That little one has been looking for the light ever since her surgery."

Sending her a puzzled glance, Rob asked, "What do you mean?"

"Her condition has been getting worse instead of better."

His heart dropped like a stone. "Can they save her?"

"They are doing everything they can."

The alarm stopped, and in the sudden silence he heard Nora calling out orders for medication and asking for a stat blood gas. Her face was calm, but her voice vibrated with intensity. After the requested drugs had been given, Nora studied the monitor intently, then turned to one of the nurses. "Why wasn't I paged?"

"I was told Dr. Kent was covering for you. I've paged him three times, but he hasn't answered."

"I want to be paged every time one of my patients is in trouble. It doesn't matter if Dr. Kent is covering or not. You call me. Is that clear?"

Meekly, the nurse nodded and said, "Yes, Doctor."

Leaning toward Theresa, Rob asked, "What's wrong with the baby?"

"She had what we call transposition of the great arteries. Think of the heart as two separate pumps fused together. The right side of the heart collects blood from the body and sends it to the lungs for oxygen. The left side of the heart collects blood from the lungs and sends it to the rest of the body."

"Okay, I get that."

"Early on, the blood vessels coming out of the top of Cara's heart began to grow incorrectly. The right side of her heart collects blood from the body but the blood vessel that should take it to the lungs lead out to the body instead. So blood leaves the heart without oxygen. The left side still collects blood from the lungs but then sends it back to the lungs again."

"Wait a minute. You can't live if your body

isn't getting oxygen. How did she survive until now?"

"The same way all babies do. In the womb. Cara got her oxygen from her mother's blood. It wasn't until after Cara was born and had to breathe on her own that the trouble began."

"I take it Dr. Blake couldn't fix her heart?"

"From what I understand, Dr. Blake did a beautiful switch of the arteries. Cara's blood is now going exactly where it should."

He shook his head. "Then why isn't she getting better?"

"Because sometimes life isn't fair, Mr. Dale. Cara suffered a stroke. Her brain is damaged. It's one of the risks involved in being put on the heart–lung bypass machine during open-heart surgery. We see a lot fewer cases like this now than we did ten years ago, but it can happen to anyone who undergoes this kind of surgery."

"What can be done for her?"

Theresa gave a deep sigh and laid a hand on his shoulder. "If you believe in prayer, pray for her recovery. Everything *humanly* possible is already being done."

Rob nodded and breathed a silent prayer for the baby and for the men and women working to save her.

The unit doors opened. A distinguished-looking man with wings of silver in his dark hair and a deep tan walked briskly toward them. His white lab coat flapped open to reveal a gray silk shirt and a red tie above well-tailored slacks. He smoothed his sleek hair with one hand as he asked, "Did someone page me?"

Theresa left Rob's side to confer softly with the man Rob assumed was the missing Dr. Kent. After listening to what the head nurse had to tell him, Dr. Kent nodded and walked into the room.

At the foot of the bed, he thrust his hands in his coat pockets. "I see you have everything under control, Nora. Is there anything I can do?"

She was reading a slip of paper from one of the machines beside the bed and didn't glance up. "We have a stable heart rhythm at the moment."

He ran a finger between his neck and his collar. "The batteries were dead in this silly pager of mine."

Nora looked up but she didn't smile. "Yes, one of the nurses mentioned she paged you several times. I find changing the batteries on a regular basis prevents such problems."

She moved away from the bed and turned to the residents who had been watching her. "Let's get started on rounds, shall we? Dr. Dalton, perhaps you can give us an overview of this patient's neurological status, and Dr. Glasgow can give us fluid recommendations."

A nervous-looking young man with thick glasses swallowed hard, then begin reciting a list of facts and numbers. Most of the nurses filed out of the room, leaving only one to answer questions posed by Nora and the other doctors. It was as if nothing special had happened. One minute Rob had been watching Cara Dempsey's life hanging by a thread and the next minute everyone had gone back to other duties. It was almost bizarre.

He turned his attention back to Nora. What kind of woman did it take to make life-and-death decisions for children like this on a regular basis? What did it take for her to do such a job? He wanted to know what kind of toll it exacted on her, how she handled the pressure, what made her tick. He wanted to learn a lot more about her—and not just for his story.

Nora clasped her arms across her middle as the adrenaline rush ebbed away, leaving her feeling weak and shaken. It took all her strength to maintain a calm, controlled demeanor. It was important for her students to see that panic had no place in a critical care setting. Getting them to focus on the details of their patient might very well prevent a crisis from occurring again.

Glancing down at Cara, Nora bit the corner of her lip. She had helped the baby cheat death once more, but would it be enough?

I want to fix her. I'm a surgeon. That is what I do. I fix broken kids.

Only some children couldn't be fixed. She knew that better than anyone. She had done all she could do for this one at the moment. She accepted it, but she didn't like it.

From the corner of her eye, she saw Rob enter the room and stand at the far edge of the group. As she listened to the young residents list the baby's treatments, she turned so that she could see Rob better without being observed.

What was he thinking? Was he looking for a story angle or was it genuine concern that she saw in his eyes when his gaze rested on the baby?

And why did she care what the man thought? Determined to put him out of her mind, she looked at the residents. "Who is next on our list?"

Rounds were accomplished in a relatively short time. As the group broke apart to attend to various other duties, Nora returned to the computer corner and started dictating her notes for the day. When she was finished, she looked over to see Rob straddling one of the office chairs nearby. His arms were crossed on the seat back and his chin rested on his forearms. He watched her intently.

"What?" she asked, growing uncomfortable with his scrutiny.

"Is Cara Dempsey going to be okay?"

"I don't know." The faces of the children who had died while under her care would never be forgotten. Their names crowded into her mind.

For a moment, she was tempted to share with him how truly difficult it was to do the job she loved. Fortunately, her pager began to beep. She checked the message. "It looks as if we are done for the day. I'll show you back to the office so you can change."

"Do you often have to save the day because Dr. Kent can't be reached?"

She scowled at him and began walking down the hall. "Of course not. We're a team."

"He isn't much of a team player if the nurses can't get ahold of him when he's needed."

As much as Nora didn't like Rob prying into her life, she wasn't about to turn him loose on Peter. Her partner had been going though a rough time of his own since his recent divorce.

"Dr. Kent's pager battery was dead. It happens. You may shadow me and ask questions about open-heart surgery or Ali Willis's care, but I will not discuss my colleagues with you. Are we clear on that?"

"Crystal clear."

"Good. I'm finished with my rounds for the day and I don't have any patients scheduled in the office. Unless you wish to sit and watch me sign insurance forms and wade through the paperwork waiting for me now, I suggest you leave."

"Okay then, I'll see you tomorrow."

"No, I won't be here." She stopped at the elevator instead of taking the stairs. Her legs were still feeling shaky. It opened quickly, and she punched the button for the third floor.

"You mean you actually get a day off? That's great. Perhaps we could get together over lunch and you could tell me more about your work with Children of the Day."

"That won't be possible. I'm working at the Fort Bonnell Medical Center tomorrow. I cover a few shifts a month there so that the army cardiac surgeons can get a little time off."

"What if there is an emergency with one of the kids in this unit?"

The elevator doors opened and she stepped out. "Dr. Kent will be covering here. My next surgery is scheduled for the day after tomorrow at 8 a.m. sharp. If you wish to join me, you should be here at six-thirty."

As they entered her office, Carmen looked up and held out a stack of notes. "You have two requests for consults. One from a doctor in Waco and one from here in Austin. Oh, and Tarkott Pharmaceuticals returned your call."

"It's about time. Get them on the line for me again."

Walking into her inner office, Nora noted with relief that Rob chose not to follow. She didn't like feeling as if she were constantly on display.

Sitting behind her desk, she turned on her computer and waited for it to boot up. The welcome screen flashed on and Nora opened the files she needed to update. Typing quickly, she had finished her first case when the phone buzzed and Carmen's voice came over the speaker. "I have Tarkott's CEO, Mr. Sawyer, on line one."

Quentin Sawyer had once worked with her husband. His reputation for being a hard businessman was well earned. This wouldn't be easy. She pressed the button. "Good morning, Quentin. Thank you for returning my call. I hope you and Merilee are enjoying the cooler weather."

She engaged in a stint of small talk in spite

of her discomfort at trying to do so. Quentin and his wife had been friends of her husband, but Nora never felt she belonged in their social circle. Still, her old contacts in the pharmaceutical world came in handy at times like this.

When Quentin paused for breath in his description of his latest classic car acquisition, Nora jumped in. "As you know from my messages, Quentin, my charity, Children of the Day, is in desperate need of antibiotics. Our doctors in one of our refugee camps have reported a severe outbreak of staphylococcus, and we are asking for your help. We need four thousand vials of penicillin, and I'm not going to take no for an answer."

Rob stood beside Carmen's desk and listened through Nora's partially open door to her side of the conversation. He might be guilty of eavesdropping, but she was talking about Children of the Day and that was his story. He smiled at the secretary and took a seat in one of the chairs just outside Nora's door as if he were waiting for her to finish.

"No," Nora said emphatically. "Five hundred vials isn't enough. We need four thousand. Your company's tax break on such a donation will more than offset the cost of sending us the drugs.

We both know the drugs are sitting in your warehouse taking up space. Your newer generation antibiotics are in much more demand."

In the silence that followed as she listened to the person on the other end of the line, Rob caught Carmen's eye. "Does she do this often?"

"All the time. She knows a lot of drug people. I think that's what her husband did before he died."

Nora's voice cut in again. "You must be joking. I'm willing to take products with less than one year's shelf life but not something that is going to expire in two months. Six months is as low as I will go, and only because I know exactly where the drugs are going and that there won't be a delay in using them. I'm sure your company wants to be seen as ethical as well as charitable." Nora's tone was cool as ice. Rob didn't envy the person on the other end of the line.

He pulled out his notebook and began to jot down some notes.

"I have a reporter here from the paper *Liberty and Justice.* You may have heard of them," Nora continued. "I'm sure you don't want them doing a story about how Tarkott Pharmaceuticals is giving away drugs that are worthless in exchange for a hefty tax break."

Rob's eyebrows rose in surprise. So she wasn't above using the power of the press when it suited her. He admired her nerve.

"Good. Send the drugs directly to me. I'll take care of the international shipping costs and the needed forms. I thank you, and Children of the Day thanks you. We'll make sure that your company is given the recognition it deserves for your kind gesture. Please give Merilee my best. Goodbye."

The sound of her receiver hitting the cradle signaled Rob that she was free. He rose to his feet, then stepped inside her office. At the sight of him, her expression hardened in a way that would have made most people turn tail. "I thought we were through for today."

"I have a couple more questions, but I couldn't help overhearing your conversation just now. Do you often solicit drugs for Children of the Day?" He flipped open his notepad and began writing.

"I help when I can."

"It must make it easier for you than for some since your husband was in the pharmaceutical business." He waited to jot down her comments, but when she didn't speak he glanced at her.

During his years in the army he had seen fear

in the eyes of many people, but he certainly wasn't expecting to see that emotion on Nora's face at this moment. Her eyes were wide with alarm, her skin drained of color.

He lowered his pen and took a step toward her. "What's wrong?"

She recoiled and looked away. "Nothing. Nothing's wrong except that you are keeping me from getting my work done. I really have to insist that you leave now." Her voice trembled ever so slightly. She pulled a folder from the stack at the side of her desk and opened it.

He stood rooted to the spot, uncertain of what to do. "I'm sorry if I upset you."

"I'm not upset. I'm simply busy."

Her tone was stronger, but he didn't believe her. Part of him wanted to know what had caused her distress, and another part of him wanted only to reassure and comfort her.

"Good day, Mr. Dale!" This time the command was unmistakable. She didn't even glance in his direction.

"Good day, Nora." He walked out of her office with a dozen unanswered questions whirling though his mind.

Calling herself every kind of fool, Nora closed the file she was holding and rubbed her temples with the tips of her fingers. The tension headache building behind her eyes didn't ease.

She had overreacted to Rob's comment about Bernard's business. She had seen the look of speculation in the reporter's eyes when he left the room. Her hopes that he wouldn't look too closely into her past might have just flown out the window and *she* had thrown up the sash. What could she do? How could she fix this?

By giving him what he wanted.

The answer that occurred to her was surprisingly simple. Rob wanted an in-depth look at her work for Children of the Day. The more she resisted his attempts to do that, the more likely he was to wonder why she wouldn't cooperate.

If she decided to help him, would he think it was strange? Would it make him more suspicious?

She glanced at Pamela's picture. What choice did she have?

Rising, she hurried to her door and pulled it open. To her relief, he hadn't left yet.

"Rob, I'm sorry," she said quickly. "I shouldn't have snapped at you."

She didn't know who looked more surprised by her apology, Rob or Carmen.

He shook his head. "Don't give it another thought. Are you sure you're okay?"

She took a step toward him. "I'm stressed, that's all. With baby Dempsey's condition on my mind and then hearing a pharmaceutical company tell me they don't want to help sick children…I just lost it. You were a handy target. I'm sorry."

"I can see how you might feel stressed."

"That's no excuse for my behavior. I do understand what you are trying to do with your article. If you can raise the awareness of what Children of the Day does, then I'll try not to hinder you." She smiled broadly. "You said you had a few more questions. I'll try to answer them."

He waved one hand. "It can wait."

"Are you sure?"

"Absolutely. I'll get out of your hair and let you get back to work."

"All right then. Good day." Nora walked back into her office and sank into her chair. She hoped that Rob had accepted her explanation and would be satisfied with that.

He watched as Nora went back inside her office and wondered why she had undergone such a change of heart. Her explanation was reasonable, but it didn't feel quite right.

He nodded to Carmen. "I'll see you the day after tomorrow. I'm going into surgery with the good doctor."

"You won't see me. Delia will be back tomorrow."

"Then I look forward to meeting Delia."

"I'm not so sure you should look forward to it. Delia is a bit of a dragon. She runs a very tight ship."

"Then I look forward to taming the dragon."

Carmen tilted her head to one side. "If anyone can do it, I think you're the man for the job."

He touched his brow with one finger and gave Carmen a wink before heading out the door. In the hallway, he glanced at his notes. He had written the words *husband, company name* and *background check.*

After pulling his cell phone from his pocket, Rob scrolled through his contacts until he found the one he was looking for. He placed the call, and on the second ring it went to voice mail.

A man's gravely voice said, "Encore Investigations. Leave a message at the tone."

"Murray, this is Rob Dale. Call me when you get this. I have a job for you. Dig up anything you can on a charity called Children of the Day in Prairie Springs, Texas."

Rob paused as he considered his next request. Was he doing the right thing by prying into Nora's past? If she was no different than any other person he was writing about, why did he feel guilty about doing this?

Maybe it was because he already felt a personal connection to her that he couldn't quite explain. He needed the information for the piece, but he also wanted to get to know more about Nora for selfish reasons. He'd never met anyone as complex, as driven, and yet with an underlying vulnerability that touched something deep inside him.

If they were simply two people getting to know each other, he wouldn't invade her privacy this way, but she was part of a story. He'd let his personal feelings get in the way of good reporting only a short time ago and it had cost him. He wouldn't make the same mistake twice.

Finally, he said, "Murray, I also want you to do a background check for me. Find out what you can about a cardiac surgeon named Dr. Nora Blake, about her deceased husband and about the company he worked for. Something tells me Dr. Blake isn't exactly what she seems."

Chapter Four

The sun was just peeking over the horizon the next morning when Nora pulled into the nearly empty parking lot at the Prairie Springs park. Only a half dozen cars dotted the spaces. Five of them she recognized as other runners who preferred to exercise in the quiet of the early morning hours. The red SUV was one she hadn't seen here before.

As she opened her car door, the beast tried to get out first, climbing over Nora in his exuberance at the idea of a run in the park. Nora held on to the leash with grim determination as fifty pounds of Airedale terrier hit the end of the nylon strap.

"Conan, stop it. Sit!" Nora commanded, getting out and rubbing the bruise she knew she'd have on her thigh.

The russet brown, curly coated dog with a black saddle marking on his back dropped to his haunches and gave her a wide doggy grin. Once they were on the jogging paths, he would be the perfectly behaved running companion, but sometimes he was too eager to get under way.

"Good dog. Stay until I've done my stretches."

The big terrier lay down to watch her. Officially, he belonged to Pamela, but his preference for Nora began the minute they brought the wiggling puppy home from the breeder.

Getting a puppy had been Nora's idea, a fact Pamela reminded her stepmother of when Conan destroyed some piece of furniture or dug up the flower beds. The only way to keep his exuberance in check was to see that he got plenty of exercise. Hence, he had become Nora's running partner.

Nora looped the leash over her wrist and quickly warmed up. Conan managed to behave until she was ready. Once her stretches were done, she looked over the park.

There were a number of trails and paths to choose from. The easiest ones meandered through the flat areas of the park that skirted the river. For the adventurous runner, there were paths that traversed the steep hillsides and rugged woodlands on the other side of the water. A narrow footbridge offered an easy way across the river.

"Okay, boy, which way today? Shall we run down by the water or up on the hill trails?"

Watching her intently, the big dog whined and then barked once.

"The river it is," Nora said, checking her watch. She didn't have to report to the Fort Bonnell hospital until ten o'clock and it was barely after six-thirty. The thought of getting away from the stress of her job and enjoying the beautiful morning made her smile. There weren't enough days like this.

With her eager companion running beside her, Nora started off at an easy pace. The morning air was cool, but it didn't feel like October. There wasn't a nip in the air yet or the smell of autumn that she had loved in her native New England. This part of Texas could have its share of cold winter weather, but so far, summer was lingering in the hill country.

She decided on a circuit that took her two miles around the outside perimeter of the park before it cut back along the river near the footbridge. The path was wide and they came upon only one other person jogging in the opposite direction. For most of the first two miles, they had the place to themselves. That was exactly how Nora liked it.

Both she and the dog were hitting a good stride when they rounded a sharp curve in the path at the footbridge. Just then a runner came off the bridge and turned in front of them. Nora veered right to go around him. Conan veered left.

The second she realized what was happening, Nora tried to stop. Conan didn't. The man they attempted to mow down jumped lightly over the taut strap leaving Nora to gape at him in astonishment as she stumbled past. It was Rob Dale.

Recovering her stride, she looked back once, then kept going. Of all the people in the world, why did she have to run into him? She'd thrown on an old yellow jersey that had seen better days and her most comfortable running pants—the faded green pair that had a hole in one knee. Maybe he hadn't recognized her.

No such luck. Within a few dozen yards, he came up from behind her.

"Morning, Nora." Matching her stride, he fell into step beside her.

"Mr. Dale." She nodded once in his direction.

"Nice morning for a run," he said, grinning from ear to ear.

"It was." Her tone was dismissive, but as usual he didn't take the hint.

Glancing at him from the corner of her eye, it was plain that he had already been at this for some time. His gray T-shirt was soaked with sweat, and his shoes and the hems of his dark blue pants were coated with fine gray dust from one of the park's steep trails that zigzagged to the top of the bluffs, yet he didn't seem winded.

Her first impression about him had been correct. He carried himself like an athlete. Although she considered trying to sprint on ahead, she doubted she could outrun him. Loping beside her, Conan eyed the man and growled low in his throat.

Good dog, she thought, mentally promising him an extra dog biscuit when they got home.

"Do you run here often?" Rob asked.

"No."

It wasn't a complete lie. She didn't get out here as frequently as she liked. She certainly wouldn't come here again until after he had left town. "I really prefer to run alone."

"Usually I do, too." There was a touch of surprise in his voice. Looking over, she met his gaze. His smile did funny things to her stomach.

Staring straight ahead once again, she considered what to do next. It was nearly two miles back to her car. He was jogging in the same direction. Other than being outright rude, she didn't know how to get rid of him. She considered just stopping and letting him go ahead, but knowing him, he probably wouldn't.

The fastest way to get rid of him was simply to keep going. She increased her stride and tried her best to ignore him.

The path they were on curved in and out of the trees that covered a large part of the park. Their long shadows kept the air cool in the early morning. A small breeze rustled the branches overhead and brushed her cheeks. The leaves of the oaks and maples were just beginning to put on their autumn colors of burnt orange, gold and red. A few fallen leaves dotted the path and grass beneath the trees. It was a beautiful area.

Normally she would have slowed her pace to enjoy the scenery, but not today. The trail made another sharp bend that brought them within sight of the river again.

The morning sunlight danced as reflected diamonds glittering off the ripples in the shallow water. On the opposite shore, a whitetail deer was drinking. The doe raised her head and then bounded away into the trees with her tail held high.

"That is what I call pretty," Rob said, glancing down at Nora with a sweet smile.

After that, he didn't say anything else. They ran side by side with only the sound of their feet hitting the ground and Conan panting beside them. Nora's self-consciousness slowly ebbed away. Bit by bit, the joy she always felt when she ran crept back over her.

When the parking lot came into sight, Rob slowed to a walk and propped both hands on his hips. To his surprise, Nora did the same. They were both breathing heavily. As they walked to cool down, he studied her covertly.

He liked that she was a runner. Without the hospital scrubs or lab coat she looked like any ordinary woman out for a jog in the park. Her blond hair was pulled back into a ponytail. Her running clothes had been chosen for comfort not style. She wasn't out here in the early hours of the morning to impress anyone. She was out here because she loved it. He understood the feeling.

When he'd had a chance to catch his breath and he could tell that she had done the same, he asked, "What's your dog's name?"

"Conan."

"Like the barbarian?"

She smiled slightly. It was the first time he'd seen her do so. He liked the way it softened her face. She should do it more often.

"That wasn't what we had in mind when we named him, but it fits."

By now they had almost reached the parking lot and Rob found himself reluctant to end the chance encounter. He dropped to one knee to retie a shoe that didn't need adjusting. Nora stopped walking. Conan apparently decided Rob didn't pose a threat and came to nuzzle his hand in the hopes of getting some attention. Rob, happy to oblige, ruffled the dog's ears. "He's a friendly fellow."

"Not usually," Nora admitted, giving him a quizzical look.

"Then I guess I feel privileged," Rob said with a chuckle as Conan began licking his face.

Rising to his feet, Rob patted the dog's head one more time. A picnic table sat nearby beneath the wide spreading branches of an oak tree. Rob took a chance and walked over to sit on the rustic planks. He held out his hand to Conan, and the dog tugged on the leash trying to reach him. Nora stepped closer.

Rob kept his attention on the dog as if it didn't matter whether or not Nora was there. Scratching Conan's wooly head just behind his ears, Rob crooned. "You're a good boy, aren't you? I'll bet you play a wicked game of fetch."

Glancing up at Nora, but keeping one hand on the dog, Rob said, "So tell me about Prairie Springs. What brought you and the barbarian to west Texas?"

Nora glanced toward her car, then back at Rob, a look of indecision on her face. In the end, her dog's delight in his new playmate seemed to win her over.

"Mercy Medical Center made me an offer I couldn't refuse," she replied.

"If you don't mind my asking, what kind of offer was that?"

She sent him a suspicious look. "Reporter Rob Dale of the *Liberty and Justice* is asking my permission before he peppers me with questions?"

He held his hands wide. "I don't have a pen or paper on me, so you're safe."

Obviously skeptical, she said, "Hmm. Maybe, but I doubt it."

He leaned back and folded his arms across his chest. "Fine. You ask the questions."

"How did you get that scar on your arm?"

He glanced at the puckered red mark. "Sorry. That would be privileged medical information."

She raised one eyebrow.

"All right. A camel kicked me."

"Is that a joke?"

"Oh, how I wish it were. Nope, a racing camel kicked me and broke my arm. It didn't heal right, so my paper brought me back to the States for surgery to break it again and pin it in place." He wiggled his fingers. "I'm almost as good as new."

She crossed her arms over her chest. "You expect me to believe that you're a camel racer in your spare time?"

He shook his head. "No. I was doing a piece on the plight of child jockeys. Kids as young as five are forced to participate in a very danger-ous sport. Some are even bought and sold as slaves."

"Yes, I've heard a little about the practice. Did you publish your article?"

"I managed to type it up with one hand."

"That's dedication. Do you think it did any good?"

"It brought some attention to the problem. I'm not sure I did much real good, but I tried."

She took a seat on the bench beside him. "That counts for something."

He was glad it did in her eyes. "My turn. Aside from money, what would make one hospital's offer better than the next?"

"Why do you think my move here wasn't about the money?"

"Your pro bono work for Children of the Day tells me money isn't a high priority for you."

"You assume that. I could have ulterior motives. Besides, until I moved here, I'd never heard of Children of the Day."

He leaned forward and propped his elbows on his knees. "Okay, I assume the best about people. It's one of my flaws, but it wasn't about the money, was it?"

"I was promised the chance to set up a pediatric cardiac program exactly as I wished."

"But?"

"Yes, there frequently is a *but* in the business part of any medical program. After I arrived, funds were not available to purchase new surgical equipment or to enlarge the PICU to handle more cases."

He frowned. "I thought the PICU head nurse told me they were planning an expansion."

"They are now. A private donation is making it possible. Given a little more time and money, I'm going to develop a pediatric cardiac surgical unit that will rival any in the country." He heard the determination in her voice and saw the resolve in her eyes.

"Is it important to be better than anyone else?"

"Austin is a rapidly growing city in a rapidly growing area of the United States. For any child born with a cardiac defect here, yes, it's important that this unit be the best."

"Then I'm sure it will happen for you. Who made the donation to your cause?"

"I don't know." Rising suddenly to her feet, she gave a gentle tug on Conan's lead. The dog moved to stand by her side.

"I'd think you'd want to find out, maybe ask them for more money."

"The money came from an anonymous donor. I really should be going," she added, looking down to avoid his gaze.

He wanted to stay awhile longer, but he knew their time had come to an end. He stood, too. At least he'd been granted the chance to get to know her outside of the hospital. "I'll see you tomorrow before surgery."

She had slipped back into her cool professional demeanor. "Yes, don't be late, Mr. Dale. I won't wait on you."

"I'll be there bright and early. You can count on it."

She walked away with her dog at her side. Rob hoped she would look back at him, but only Conan spared him a backward glance.

Chapter Five

Nora rolled over and switched off her alarm a minute before the buzzer was due to sound. Sleep had been hard to come by last night, and not just because she couldn't get Rob Dale out of her mind. Her late-night emergency surgery had driven away every thought of him for a time, but when she returned home he had crept back into her mind.

As much as she tried to tell herself that she didn't relish the idea of spending any more time in his company, some small part of her was looking forward to showing him her work. Surgery was her passion. She loved it and she wanted him to understand that.

If only she didn't have to be careful about revealing too much of herself. He was very good at his job and that made him dangerous to her peace of mind.

Rising, she pulled on a red chintz robe over her simple white cotton nightgown. After making her bed, she padded barefoot down the polished wooden stairs. The smell of cinnamon toast and freshly brewed coffee reached her before she rounded the corner into the gleaming, ultramodern kitchen.

Pamela, her 24-year-old stepdaughter, sat at the oval walnut table situated in front of a large bay window that overlooked the lawn and garden at the back of the house. She glanced up from the newspaper spread out in front of her and tucked a lock of brown hair back behind her ear. Conan was lying under the table, happily gnawing on a chew toy.

Nora walked up to Pamela, slipped her arms around her shoulders and hugged her tightly, then dropped a kiss on her head. "Have I told you lately how much I love you?"

"Every day and twice on Sunday. I'm sorry one of your patients died."

Nora swallowed the lump in her throat. "What makes you think I lost a patient?"

Pamela patted Nora's arms still entwined about her shoulders. "I know this fierce hugging and that tone in your voice. It's a sign things didn't…go well."

Nora straightened. With one hand she smoothed Pamela's hair. "I'm as transparent as glass to you, aren't I? You're up early. What's the occasion?"

"I knew you had surgery today and if I wanted to see you at all, it would have to be at breakfast. There's toast and coffee if you want some. Do you want to talk about what happened at the hospital last night?"

Nora tried never to burden Pamela with the unhappy side of her work. "No, but thanks for the offer. Did you need to see me about something special?"

"No, I just like to spend time with you, and the busier you get at the hospital, the harder that becomes."

"I know. I'm sorry." Nora moved to the counter and poured the dark brew into a thick brown mug. She added a hearty dollop of cream from the carton in the refrigerator and carried her cup to the table, where she sat down opposite Pamela.

"Don't be sorry," Pamela said quickly. "I know you're doing what you love and I'm happy your practice is growing."

Nora managed a smile but decided to change

the subject. "How is your new job at the library working out?"

"Good. Margaret Porter is a dream to work for. She's really open to new ideas for the youth and children's section. When she found out that I sometimes volunteer for Children of the Day, she asked me to look into coordinating some of the library's services with theirs. Are you sure you're okay? You don't look like you slept at all."

Nora blew on her coffee and then took a sip. She didn't want to depress Pamela by discussing her work. Setting her mug down, she said, "I slept, but I'll sleep better when that reporter is gone. I still can't believe that he went over my head to get permission to go into surgery with me today."

"I need to meet this guy."

Frowning at Pamela's wide grin, Nora said, "Why on earth would you want to meet him? He is the most annoying, nosey, pushy, smug man on the face of the earth." She picked up a wedge of toast and took a large bite, preferring to ignore the fact that she hadn't found him annoying at the park yesterday.

"Any man who gets this kind of rise out of you is definitely worth knowing."

"And what is that supposed to mean?" Nora mumbled.

"It means that I had just about given up hope."

After swallowing hard, Nora demanded, "Hope of what?"

"Hope that you would meet a man who sparked some kind of interest from you. I know that you loved Dad, but he's been gone for six years now. Don't you think it's time you started dating again? You don't have to spend your life alone."

Nora had no intention of looking for another relationship. She wasn't willing to risk her heart again. The knowledge of Bernard's betrayal was a bitter memory, but one she would never share with her stepdaughter. Pamela had adored her father. After his death, Nora had done everything in her power to protect the grieving teenager, including keeping the truth well hidden. "I don't ever intend to marry again. I'm content with my life as it is."

"It's not like I'm going to be living here forever. I'd like to think that you'll have someone to look after you and to love you when I'm not around."

Nora opened her mouth and then closed it again. Shocked, she reached across the table to take Pamela's hand. "Honey, you don't need to stay with me. If you want to get your own place, I would miss you, but I would understand. I don't need someone to look after me."

Pamela leaned back and crossed her arms. "Really? What day does the trash get picked up?"

"I don't know—Friday—it gets picked up on Friday."

"Tuesday. How soon will the oil need to be changed in your car?"

"What difference does that make?"

"Fifteen hundred more miles. Your work is the whole focus of your life, Nora. You need someone who will notice the details outside of the hospital."

"I can learn to do those things."

Pamela arched one eyebrow. "You're thirty-five years old. If you were going to learn to do those things you would know how by now."

"You don't need to make it sound like I'm some decrepit old dog that can't learn a few new tricks."

Pamela smiled that pixie grin that had won Nora's heart the very first day they had met. "You aren't old, and I don't think that you're decrepit. I just know how you are. Even dad used to say that if it didn't have to do with medicine, you didn't think it mattered. You have a one-track mind."

"I'll hire a housekeeper if that will make you feel better, but I'm not going to go looking for a husband just so he'll know what day to take out my trash."

Leaning forward, Pamela stretched her hand palm up. Without hesitation, Nora took hold of it. "Medicine matters, but there is more to life than work. I wish you could see that. I know you still grieve for Sondra and for Dad, but it's not too late to start another family of your own."

Nora felt her stomach drop. Sometimes she still dreamed about the sweet smell of her baby girl nestled in her arms, but when she opened her eyes, she faced reality with a grim determination. This was her life now.

"Pamela, you and Conan are the only family I want or need."

The younger woman squeezed Nora's hand. "Maybe that's true, but I can't help thinking that there is someone out there who will love you as you deserve to be loved. Not as a great stepmom, which you are, or as a great surgeon, but as a woman."

When Rob walked out of the lobby and into the parking lot of the Prairie Springs Inn, the eastern sky held only a hint of pink and gold on a few wisps of high clouds. The air was still cool but the day promised to be another hot one. October in the hill country of west Texas was a lot different than October in Washington, DC. As he drew in a deep breath of clean air,

Rob decided that he liked it here better than he liked the congested capitol.

Stepping into his red Jeep Cherokee truck, he soon put the small town behind him. Past the city limits, the dawn highlighted the steep bluffs and hills with a clear golden light that was so beautiful he couldn't help being overwhelmed by the sight.

What a wondrous day You have made, Lord. Thank You for this gift. Help me to use it wisely.

Rob sped toward Austin with his windows rolled down, enjoying the brief sights of the country and a short conversation with God before the outskirts of the city began to clutter the view.

As he pulled into the hospital parking lot, he checked his watch and saw that he still had twenty minutes before presurgical rounds in the PICU were due to start. If he stopped by Nora's office he might have a chance to spend a few minutes alone with her before her hectic day got under way. He tried telling himself it was a good angle for his story, but the truth was—he simply wanted to see her.

In spite of their differences, Nora drew him in in a way no woman ever had before. She was special. He sensed it deep in his soul. God had brought them together for reasons Rob didn't understand, but he was eager to explore the feelings she evoked. Whistling a favorite old tune, he entered the building and took the elevator to the third floor.

The office door was unlocked. He knocked once and then walked in. A thin woman with sparse brown hair and garish red lipstick sat behind the reception desk. She scowled at him. "May I help you?"

He grinned. "You must be Delia."

"I am *Miss* Walden—and you are?" She arched one eyebrow, her frosty tone making him feel like an errant six-year-old.

He held out his hand. "I'm Robert Dale, reporter for the *Liberty and Justice*. Would you tell Nora that I'm here?"

She slowly withdrew a pencil from the holder at the front of her desk, ignoring his outstretched fingers. "*Doctor Blake* isn't in the office, Mr. Dale. Would you care to leave a message?"

He let his arm drop. "No, I'll just wait for her in her office."

"That isn't possible. No one is allowed access to either Dr. Kent or Dr. Blake's offices unless they are present."

"Of course. I'll wait out here, then. How was Las Vegas?"

"It was hot." She turned to her computer and

proceeded to ignore him. He settled onto one of the chairs along the wall. He had rarely met a woman he couldn't charm, but Delia Walden was apparently made of stern stuff.

"Have you worked here a long time, Miss Walden?"

She continued to type. He listened to the rapid clack of her nails on the keyboard. After a moment, he sat forward and spoke louder. "Have you worked here long, Miss Walden?"

She stopped typing and the printer began to spew out pages. When it finished, she gathered them together, rose and carried them into Dr. Kent's office. A minute later, she returned empty handed, sat down and started typing again.

Rob glanced at the clock. It was past time for rounds to begin. Nora struck him as a very punctual person. He hoped nothing was wrong. "Is it unusual for Dr. Blake to be this late?"

Delia didn't pause. "Dr. Blake is not late. She came in half an hour ago."

He rose to his feet. "She did? Then where is she?"

"She normally goes to medical records to review old charts first thing in the morning. She should be making rounds in the PICU now."

Great. Now he was the one who was late. "I wish you had told me that when I came in."

Delia stopped working and gave him a cold smile. "You didn't ask me where she was."

Pressing his lips into a tight line, he nodded, then said, "I'll be more specific in the future, Miss Walden."

She turned away. "I'm sure you will."

He left the office and hurried down the hallway toward the pediatric wing. At the PICU, he pressed the button on the wall and the doors swung open. A group of nurses and doctors were already clustered at the front desk. As Rob walked down the hall toward them, he glanced into Cara Dempsey's room and stopped short.

The bed was empty. The jumble of monitors and pumps were gone, leaving only the warming bed covered with a crisp white sheet sitting against the wall. A cold feeling settled in his chest.

The automatic doors opened behind him and Nora came striding into the unit. He turned to her and asked, "Where is Cara?"

"She's gone." Nora's voice was so matter-of-fact that for a second he thought he hadn't heard her correctly. She walked past him without pausing.

Stunned, he glanced into the empty room. Deep, aching sorrow rushed in to fill his heart. God had a purpose for every soul. Only He knew what purpose Cara had served in her short life.

With leaden feet, Rob followed Nora to where she stood reading through another child's chart. He asked, "When did it happen?"

Nora didn't look up. "Late yesterday. I'm going to see the patient with the AV canal and then I'm going to scrub in for surgery. Do you still plan on joining me?"

He reached out and grabbed her arm. "Are you really so cold hearted? A child died. A child you operated on. Don't you feel anything?"

She glared at him. "What are you talking about?"

"I'm talking about Cara Dempsey."

Her lips pressed into a tight line for a second, then she said, "Cara Dempsey didn't die. Dr. Kent transferred her back to the hospital where she came from at her parents' request yesterday evening. There wasn't anything more that we could do for her here."

Relief swept through him. "She didn't die? I saw the empty bed and I thought…one of the nurses said she wasn't going to make it."

"No, she didn't die, but if she had, what I *feel* wouldn't matter, Mr. Dale."

She pulled away from his grasp and pointed down the hall. "I have another patient depending on me. A family in that room is putting their baby's life in my hands in the hope that I can give their son what they can't—a chance at a normal, healthy life."

"I made a rash assumption. I'm sorry."

"Yes, you did. Every child I see deserves my complete and utter concentration. I can't afford the luxury of *feelings* when I'm working."

Quietly, he said, "That must be very difficult for you."

For the briefest instant, her mask of indifference slipped. He saw pain and sorrow in her beautiful hazel eyes. A second later, her implacable demeanor was back in place. She took a step away and said, "Please excuse me. I have rounds to make."

Rob stood rooted to the spot as she walked away. He had been a soldier. He'd had to suppress his emotions during the heat of battle and mourn his fallen friends later when no one was depending on him to make quick, sound decisions. He thought that mindset belonged only in the jungles and deserts where armed conflicts reigned.

As he watched Nora lead the group of doctors and nurses into a room at the end of the hall, he saw the truth with sudden clarity. Nora was on her way into yet another life-and-death battle. He had no right to judge her.

Rob knew how to blend into the background. His years in the army had taught him that skill, and he put it to use that morning. After changing into scrubs, he followed Nora, Dr. Kent and several other doctors into the hallowed halls of the operating theater.

He wanted to be at Nora's elbow, probing into the emotions and drive that made her choose this kind of work, but he held back. He didn't want to distract her. He didn't want to add any pressure to her today. Instead, he watched in quiet amazement as she, along with Dr. Kent and several others, began the operation.

Dressed in bulky gowns with their faces covered by masks, it was only possible to tell the two physicians apart by their height. Both Nora and Dr. Kent donned long lenses on heavy-looking headsets that appeared awkward and cumbersome, but in his research the night before, Rob had read that the lighted magnifying loupes were essential to working on minuscule blood vessels.

There were three nurses in the room who were moving about but not directly involved in the surgery. When one seemed free, he asked her to explain what was going on.

"Dr. Blake is closing an abnormal opening

between the two chambers on the left side of the heart. To do this she has to build a wall out of living tissue and make a valve that works."

"That sounds complicated."

"It's like working on the inside of a deflated ball smaller than an egg. What sounds complicated about that?"

Rob suspected that he amused the nurse, but he couldn't tell if she was smiling behind her mask.

"Would you let Dr. Blake operate on your kid?"

"In a heartbeat. She has the gift."

"What gift is that?"

"When she makes those tiny stitches with sutures finer than a human hair, she is able to know how they will look when the heart is full and round and pumping blood again. Believe me, it's a God-given talent."

"Dr. Blake told me she doesn't believe in God."

"Maybe not, but He believes in her."

The nurse was called away and Rob moved closer to where Nora was working. Even from only a few feet away he couldn't see much. The patient was simply too small, the incision even smaller. The numerous hands holding instruments, gauzes and needles obscured any hope of his getting to view Nora's actual work.

What he did instead was observe the way the people working spoke quietly back and forth.

There was chitchat between Dr. Kent and the anesthesiologist about Dr. Kent's new sports car and his upcoming trip to Grand Cayman. The nurses talked about their kids and complained about the extra shift they were being asked to cover. From time to time, a nurse left the room to update the parents waiting down the hall. Everyone seemed on friendly terms with everyone else. Everyone exchanged bits and pieces of their lives.

Everyone, that was, except Nora.

She didn't look up; she didn't join in the chatter. If she spoke it was to direct someone or to ask for another suture or to have the lights adjusted. She seemed to Rob to be literally alone in the room—as if she were in some kind of bubble—exempt from everything except the task of mending a tiny flawed heart beneath her hands.

Nora knew Rob was there at the edge of the room. Even when he wasn't in her line of sight, she felt his presence. He wasn't being intrusive and she was grateful for that. It was hard enough to concentrate with so little sleep and with her unsuccessful surgery last night on the terminally ill soldier at the base hospital still fresh in her mind.

She had only been covering a call for the base cardiac surgeon, as she occasionally did, to help the overstretched staff at the Fort Bonnell Medical Center. The patient, a 64-year-old major, had been unconscious when she arrived. To her deep regret, she never spoke to him, only to his grieving family.

Now, exhaustion pulled at Nora but she willed it away. She couldn't afford the distraction. This patient, the one on the table, deserved her full attention. As the time passed, she eventually forgot about Rob, last night's surgery and how tired she was.

Each miniature stitch she placed with near perfection filled her with a wellspring of satisfaction. With all its stress and pain, this was her life's work and she loved it.

When the reconstruction was complete and she was satisfied that she had done her absolute best, she spoke to the perfusion technologist. "Warm him up."

As the temperature of the patient rose, she waited with bated breath for that first quiver that would signal the heart was working. It was only a few minutes, but it seemed like hours.

Then, there it was, the first contraction, followed by another and then another. Soon the tiny heart was beating briskly before her eyes.

Suddenly her exhaustion came rushing in. She stepped back from the table. "Dr. Kent, will you close, please?"

"Certainly. You've done the hard part. Take a break."

She arched her back, trying to stretch tight muscles that ached in protest. Unplugging her loupes, she walked out of the operating room and into the scrub area. After pulling off her gloves, mask and cap, she tossed them into the trash. Then she ran her fingers through her hair plastered to her temples with sweat.

"How did it go?"

She spun around, surprised to see that Rob was still there. "It went well. It was a good repair."

"Are you finished?"

She turned to the sink and began to wash her hands. "Not until we get little Mr. Drake back to the PICU and stabilized and I've had a chance to talk to his parents."

"You called him by his name. That's the first time I've heard you refer to one of your patients by name. You usually refer to them by their diagnosis."

"Do I?"

"You don't want to become emotionally involved with your patients. You see it as a weakness."

She would have to add perceptive to his list of personality traits. Pulling a paper towel from the dispenser, she leaned back against the sink and dried her hands. "I'm very tired. Can we continue this conversation some other time?"

"Sure. I just wanted to say that I admire what you do. Watching you today was awe inspiring."

He seemed so sincere. She wasn't sure exactly what to make of this about face. He had gotten her used to expecting wisecracks, not compliments. An uncomfortable silence stretched between them.

Finally, she said, "Thank you." She didn't know what else to say.

"No, thank you, Dr. Blake, for allowing me to see what it is you do. I hope I can convey even a small part of the amazing talent and patience I saw today to my readers."

"I'm glad I could be of some help."

"I'll be interviewing other people who work for Children of the Day as well as Ali and his grandfather over the next several days, so I'll be out of your hair until the day of Ali's surgery."

"Oh." How could she feel disappointed? She should be delighted—only she wasn't.

He smiled and touched one finger to his

forehead in that silly salute that he used so often. "See you around, Doc."

As he walked out of the room, Nora couldn't explain the sense of loss that weighed her down.

Chapter Six

Rob adjusted his rearview mirror to check that his tie was straight. He turned his face one way and then the other to make sure that his shave was close enough and that his normally unruly hair had been brushed into submission.

Satisfied that he would pass even the most stringent inspection, he stepped out of his truck and headed up the walk leading to a stately redbrick Georgian home just off Veteran's Boulevard in the historical district of Prairie Springs. He glanced at his watch when he reached the front door. It was ten o'clock. He was right on time. Lifting the heavy ring in the brass lion's mouth, he knocked twice.

The door opened to reveal a stern-looking white-haired man in a short-sleeved olive-green shirt and black pants. Repressing the urge to snap to attention and salute, Rob extended his hand instead.

"Good morning, sir. I'm Robert Dale from the *Liberty and Justice*. We spoke on the phone yesterday afternoon. I'd like to say how much I appreciate your sharing your grandson's story."

The older man's keen blue eyes seemed to make a quick assessment, then he nodded. "At first I thought it was a bunch of nonsense making such a fuss about it, but a lot of good men and women worked long and hard to get my boy here. They deserve the thanks, not me. I only granted this interview so that I could give credit where credit is due."

"I understand."

General Marlon Willis let out a deep breath and stepped back from the door. "All right. Come in and let's get this over with. Ali is on the sofa in the living room. He tires easily so if I say we're done, we're done. Is that clear?"

"Crystal clear, sir."

The general lead the way across the polished oak floors of the entry and into a sunny room filled with oversized and comfortable-looking furniture. Rob saw a woman with shoulder-length chestnut hair seated in a wooden ladder-back chair beside a beige couch. On the sofa, a small boy of five lay propped up with pillows. He was engaged in putting the pieces of a simple wooden jigsaw puzzle together on the low table drawn up close beside him.

The woman looked up and graced Rob with a warm and friendly smile. The general said, "Sarah, this is Rob Dale. Mr. Dale, this is my neighbor, Sarah Alpert. Sarah has been helping me keep Ali entertained."

Rising, Sarah held out her hand. "Howdy, Mr. Dale. It's a pleasure to meet y'all."

His big hand almost swallowed hers. "That accent tells me you aren't a military transplant."

"No, indeed. I'm a Texan, born and bred and mighty proud of it."

"Sarah was friends with Ali's father—my son, Greg—when they were younger." Rob didn't miss the catch in the old man's voice.

Sarah gave him a kindly smile. "He was a fine man. A bit pigheaded at times, but I have an idea who he inherited that trait from."

The general managed a ghost of a smile at her teasing. "It must have been from his mother's side of the family."

She chuckled. "Right. And pigs fly, too. At least Ali didn't inherit the family flaw. He's a perfect little gentleman."

The boy watched Rob shyly. With his dark

hair and soulful dark eyes it was obvious he was of Middle Eastern descent. Rob already knew part of the boy's history. He knew that the boy's father had been an American soldier and that his mother had been a humanitarian worker for Children of the Day in her native land.

Their marriage had caused a rift between General Willis and his son that had never healed. After his son's death when Ali was three years old, the general still didn't acknowledge his grandson. It wasn't until after a roadside bomb killed Ali's mother that the general stepped in. With the aid of Children of the Day, he arranged for his injured grandson to come to the United States.

Rob moved closer to the boy and said, *"Sabah alkair, Ali."*

Ali sat bolt upright, a bright smile wreathing his face. *"Sabah alnur."* He returned Rob's greeting and then launched into rapid Arabic.

Rob laughed and held up one hand. "You'll have to go more slowly. I'm a little rusty."

"I talk English okay good," Ali said proudly.

"Probably better than I speak Arabic," Rob conceded.

Sarah brought over a second chair. After nodding his thanks, Rob took a seat and pulled out his notepad. Smiling at the boy, he said,

"Do you mind if I ask you some questions about your trip to America?"

Ali sank back against the pillows. The animation left his face, and Rob noticed how pale he looked. The general sat on the end of the sofa and patted the boy's leg. "It's all right if you don't want to talk about it."

Ali lifted his chin and Rob saw a likeness between the boy and his grandfather in the stubborn jut of their jaws. "I can talk now. After bomb kill Om…" He paused and cast Rob an imploring look.

Rob supplied the word the boy was searching for. "Mother."

"Yes, after bomb kill my m…mother, I go to hospital in big tent."

Pressing a hand to his chest, Ali continued. "I hurt here very much. I scared until I see Dr. Mike."

Rob looked from his notes to General Willis. "Dr. Mike?"

It was Sarah who spoke first. "Captain Michael Montgomery is a U.S. Army doctor. He and Greg served together. After Greg's death, Michael kept an eye on Ali and his mother."

Something in the way she said the name Michael made Rob look at her closely. Her eyes met his briefly, then slid away. A faint blush tinted her fair cheeks. He wondered what history she shared with the good doctor stationed so far from Texas. He didn't have a chance to speculate further because Ali spoke again.

"Dr. Mike, he say I must go America to fix my heart. He say my jadd…my grandfather, is here and he will take care of me."

He puffed out his little chest. "I tell Dr. Mike I can take care of me okay good. He say I fly in big helicopter with David and pretty nurse Maddie."

Marlon said, "Chief Warrant Office David Ryland and nurse Madeline Bright were returning to the Fort Bonnell after their tour of duty in the Middle East ended. I pulled a few strings to make sure that Ali had their company on the way back. It was the least I could do for the boy. If I had tried to do more for him and his mother sooner, perhaps none of this would have happened."

The general grew quiet as he became lost in thought. Rob caught a glimpse of the toll the old man's grief and regrets had taken on him. Compelled to offer what comfort he could, Rob said, "You are doing the best for Ali now. That's what's important. The past can't be changed."

The general nodded, then grimaced and

rubbed his left arm. Sarah leaned toward him. "Are you all right?"

He straightened and glanced at his grandson. Ali's eyes were wide with worry. Marlon managed a smile as he reached out and squeezed Ali's big toe. "I'm okay good. You go on with your story."

Ali grinned and stretched his arms wide. "After I get off helicopter, I fly in big, big plane."

"You must have been scared to come so far," Rob suggested.

"A little—but not much. Nurse Maddie and David, they stay with me. They tell me everything be fine."

"And they were right," Sarah said. "God brought you to us to get well."

"And to bring a little bit of my son back to me," Marlon added.

Rob glanced at the general. "Can I ask why Ali hasn't had the surgery already?"

"Apparently this type of injury is extremely rare. The hope at first was that the tear inside Ali's heart might heal on its own, but Dr. Montgomery wanted him in the States if that didn't happen. He was right about that. It wasn't long before the boy began having trouble with fluid on his lungs."

Sarah leaned forward to ruffle Ali's hair.

"Once he got here, Dr. Blake wanted his nutritional status improved before she scheduled his surgery. Then we had a delay because of an upper respiratory infection. Once that was cleared up and he put on some weight, the surgery was scheduled for the middle of next week."

Ali smiled at his grandfather. "Soon, Dr. Blake make me all better and we tell Nurse Tilda go away."

Marlon and Sarah laughed.

"Tilda is the home health nurse looking after Ali and me," Marlon explained. "She would have made a fine drill sergeant. She loves ordering us around."

Ali grimaced and made a sour face. "Her medicine taste very bad."

Rob chuckled, but in his mind he prayed that Nora would be able to fix Ali's damaged heart. The case of little Cara had driven home just how risky such a surgery could be.

Please, Lord, this boy has seen so much of sorrow. Let Your light shine upon him. If it is Your will, bring health, comfort and joy into his life and into the lives of those who love him.

Nora, with Pamela beside her, climbed the steps of the converted slate blue Victorian house that had become home to the charity Children of the Day. The charity was the brain child of Russian-born immigrant Anna Terenkov and named from the Bible passage 1 Thessalonians 5:5, "Ye are all the children of light, and the children of the day: we are not of the night, nor of darkness."

The organization had grown from its humble beginnings in Anna and her mother Olga's living room into a business that employed a full-time staff and had taken over the entire lower level of the building.

As Nora and Pamela crossed the wide, welcoming porch that wrapped around the gracious old home, Nora said, "You don't have to come with me if you have other things to do, Pamela. I wanted to visit with Anna about the medicine I'm shipping overseas. I don't know how long I'll be. It depends on what Anna is involved in at the moment. You can go on and I'll call your cell phone when I'm done."

"I don't mind the detour. Besides, Olga wasn't at the church this afternoon. I'm hoping to find her here so we can firm up plans for the children's traveling book exchange at her grief center. Oh, there she is."

Nora followed Pamela's gaze to see Olga sitting on the cushion-filled porch swing at the side of the house. She wasn't alone. Laura

Dean, the secretary, and Caitlin Villard, the care coordinator for Children of the Day sat beside her. Nora's stomach did a funny little flip-flop when she recognized Rob leaning against the porch railing, pen and notebook in hand as he faced the three women.

Just then, he looked over and met Nora's gaze. His face lit up with a grin that turned her tummy flutters into a full blown twister.

She bit her lip and looked away. Her reaction was absolutely irrational. She couldn't be excited to see him. The man was a nuisance, nothing more. But if that were true, then why was she standing here feeling like a high school freshman who had just been noticed by the captain of the football team?

"Whoa, who is the handsome guy smiling at you?" Pamela's curious voice cut into Nora's jumbled thoughts.

"He isn't smiling at me," Nora insisted sharply.

"Okay, then who is the handsome guy smiling at me?"

"That is the reporter I was telling you about. Ignore him."

"Not a chance. Come introduce me." Pamela tugged on Nora's arm.

"No. I have to speak to Anna. Besides, he isn't the kind of person you should know," she whispered, hoping he couldn't hear that they were talking about him. The man was conceited enough.

"You make him sound like an ax murderer. I'm more intrigued by the minute. He's coming this way. Why, Nora, I do believe you're blushing."

Her stepdaughter's amusement was more than Nora could bear. "I am not."

Pulling open the door, Nora escaped into the lobby and all but bolted through Anna's open office door.

Rob worked to overcome the pang of disappointment he felt as Nora disappeared into the building without even speaking to him. It was crazy, but he was hurt by her obvious rejection.

When the young woman with her came toward him, he recognized her from the picture on Nora's desk. Smiling, she held out her hand. "Hello, I'm Pamela Blake. Nora tells me you are exactly the kind of man I shouldn't meet."

Taken aback by her comment, he found himself at a loss for words.

She laughed at the look of confusion on his face. "I need to speak to Olga for a few minutes, then I'm going to grill you about your intentions toward my stepmother."

He found his voice. "My intentions are

strictly honorable." His conscience gave a small twinge. That wasn't exactly the whole truth.

"Nora is usually a good judge of character, so why doesn't she like you?"

He shoved his hands in the front pockets of his jeans. "I'm doing a story about Ali Tabiz Willis and Children of the Day. Your mother doesn't like the idea of anyone profiting from the suffering of children. My boss and her boss see it differently."

Pamela gave him a long, hard look. He couldn't tell what she was thinking.

"Interesting. If you're busy with Olga, I can wait and speak with her some other time."

"Mrs. Terenkov and I were almost done."

They began walking back to the porch swing where the other women sat. The wide veranda, surrounded by towering magnolias and lush crape myrtles, overlooked the street but gave the illusion of being a quiet oasis.

"You promised to call me Olga," the older woman chided in her lilting Russian accent. Dressed in a peasant blouse and full denim patchwork skirt over black and silver cowboy boots, the gregarious woman watched them with unabashed curiosity. "Hello, Pamela. How are you? How is the new job? How is your mother?"

"Fine, fine, and okay, I think." Pamela leaned

back against the rail and tucked a windblown lock of hair behind her ear.

Rob sat on the wide porch railing beside her. From his spot he kept one eye on the door, hoping to have a word with Nora before she left.

Caitlin leaned forward, "Pamela, I see you have met Mr. Dale. He's doing an article on Children of the Day for the *Liberty and Justice* newspaper."

"Maybe more than one," he admitted. "I'm finding the charity has more facets than I first expected."

"My Anna-bug, she helps everywhere she can," Olga said with obvious maternal pride.

Caitlin patted Olga's knee. "She has her mother's boundless energy."

Laura, the slim young blonde, flashed him a wide smile. "Did we tell you that Olga runs the grief counseling center at the Prairie Springs Christian Church, helps here and still finds time to run the church's singles program?"

"Really?" He made a note of the fact.

Beside him, Pamela asked, "Are you married, Mr. Dale?"

"No," he replied slowly. He wasn't quite sure what to make of the outspoken young woman, but he suspected that given some time, he would come to like her.

Pamela's smile widened. "You should drop by our singles meeting while you're in town. We meet every Thursday night. You would have a great time."

"You and Gary Bellman seemed to be having a great time together last week," Caitlin said with a wink. Rob had already learned that Caitlin, the newest staff member of Children of the Day, was the care coordinator and the woman responsible for getting Ali to the States.

Pamela blushed. "Thanks to Olga's matchmaking skills, I think I've found a winner. Now, Caitlin, I saw you and Chaplain Steve looking very cozy at the church social with the twins the other day."

"He's a wonderful man and the girls adore him," Caitlin replied with a soft smile.

Olga reached out and tweaked Caitlin cheek. "The girls aren't the only ones who adore him."

"Have you managed to get Pastor Fields to ask you out, yet, Olga?" Caitlin's deft turning of the tables impressed Rob who knew she had been a successful lawyer before returning to her home town of Prairie Springs to care for her recently orphaned nieces.

"Yes, he asked me out last night."

Laura's eyes widened in disbelief. "He did?"

Pamela squealed with delight and clapped her hands. "Tell us everything."

Clasping both hands to her chest, Olga closed her eyes and leaned back in the swing. "I was so stunned I think I said no, and then yes, yes, yes."

She pressed the back of her hand to her forehead in a dramatic gesture. "I was so nervous I thought I might faint."

She sounded more like a giddy teenager than a mature woman in her midfifties. Everyone, including Rob, laughed at her antics.

"When are you going out? Where is he taking you?" demanded Pamela, grinning from ear to ear.

Rob smiled as he glanced between the women all offering tips for the upcoming date. He had no idea that discussing what to wear and where to go could generate such enthusiastic conversations. After a few minutes he was feeling like a fish out of water until Olga turned to him.

"Mr. Dale, tell us, where do you suggest we go? I'd like to hear a man's opinion of what makes the perfect first date."

Suddenly, all eyes were on him. A fish out of water didn't quite cover the sensation creeping over him. A giraffe up to its chin in quicksand would be more like it.

He hadn't dated much in the past few years.

His life as a covert scout for the army didn't lend itself to romantic evenings. After he'd left the army, there had always been another to story to uncover and deadlines to make.

Thankfully, the front door opened and Nora came out with Anna beside her. Anna carried a tray loaded with glasses of iced tea. "The weather is so lovely I thought we would join you out here. I have great news, everyone. Dr. Blake has been able to obtain the antibiotics so desperately needed in the refugee camp in El Almira. The drugs are on their way as we speak."

"Praise the Lord," Olga cried joyously.

"Amen," Anna replied. "He certainly knew what He was doing when He sent you to our organization, Nora."

After setting the tray on a small rattan table by the swing, Anna began handing out the glasses. "What was all the squealing and laughing about? We heard you clear into my office."

"Pastor Fields asked your mother for a date," Caitlin said with glee.

Anna's eyes widened. "Oh?"

"I was going to tell you this evening, Anna." Olga's eyes slid away from her daughter's and focused on Rob. "Mr. Dale was just telling us what a man thinks would be the perfect first date."

Rob glanced at all the women waiting for his nonexistent expertise. His collar seemed uncomfortably tight. He reached for a glass of iced tea while stalling for an answer. When his gaze met Nora's he saw the faintest trace of a smile tugging at the corner of her oh-so-kissable mouth. She was enjoying his discomfort.

What would the perfect first date with her be like? Suddenly, he could see them together with amazing clarity and he liked what he saw.

Pamela said, "Dinner and a movie are always a good place to start."

"I'd take her on a hike," he said softly.

"A hike?" Olga looked at him askance.

"We'd go somewhere up into the foothills just before dawn when the air is cool and clear. At the top of a high bluff I'd spread a picnic blanket on the ground. Then, we'd share a thermos of coffee and a loaf of French bread. The kind that has that wonderful thick crust but is soft as butter on the inside, and we'd cover our bread with big spoonfuls of strawberry jam.

"Then we would watch the sun come up. We'd sit in quiet awe and hold hands as God painted the sky and the hills with breathtaking colors and opened a new day for just the two of us."

As he stared into Nora's eyes the people and things around him faded away until all he saw was her. The afternoon breeze played with the few strands of her hair that had escaped from the silver clip at the nape of her neck. He didn't know much about fashion, but her bright pink blouse made her look young and carefree—something her white lab coat and scrubs never did.

Her eyes, so recently crinkled with amusement, stared back at him now filled with an emotion he couldn't read. The connection between them was real and powerful. She broke the contact by looking away first. The rest of the world snapped back into focus for him.

Rob realized the other women were watching him with varying degrees of puzzlement, and in Pamela's case, speculation.

Olga broke the silence. "Ya, I think dinner and a movie is the place to start."

Feeling more than a little foolish, Rob said, "Dinner is great as long as you pick a place that serves a good steak even if you're only getting a salad.

"As for the movie, don't choose a chick flick on the first date. A lot of guys really don't get them. Pick a comedy or a good action thriller. If you can stand it, go for the scary movie and hide your face against his shoulder at all the good parts. Nothing makes a guy feel more macho."

His eyes were drawn to Nora again, but she wouldn't look at him. Instead, she said, "I need more ice in my tea."

Once more she escaped from his sight into the building, but Rob knew she had to come out sooner or later.

Another thing he knew for certain—Nora Blake was definitely a woman worth waiting for.

Chapter Seven

Nora hurried through the lobby and made her way straight to the small kitchen the staff used at the rear of the building. Once inside the swinging door, she put her glass down on the counter and pressed her palms to her burning cheeks.

How did he do that? How did he mesmerize her with his eyes? Try as she might, she couldn't deny that there was an attraction between them.

The bad thing was—she knew he felt it, too.

The notion that a man like Rob Dale might find her attractive wasn't beyond the bounds of belief. She'd had her share of interest from men, but other than Bernard, none of them had made an effort to get past her prickly defenses. Usually, all it took was for her to start talking about open-heart surgery to turn a first date into a final one.

So why was Rob so interested in her? Was it because he sensed she was hiding something? If he was a good reporter, and she suspected that he was, then she couldn't rule out the idea that he had ulterior motives.

If that was the case, she wouldn't fall for his obvious ploy to gain her favor.

And if that wasn't the case?

She bit her thumbnail. If she secretly longed for someone to share the joys and burdens of her life, was that wrong? She wasn't dead. Would it hurt to explore her feelings for him?

The rational part of her mind quickly squashed the glimmer of romance she felt blooming. There was no future for them. He would be gone soon. If she let down her guard where he was concerned, it would only bring her disappointment and heartache.

I need to avoid him until he finishes his story and leaves town.

Even as the thought occurred to her, she knew it wasn't going to happen. He would be at the hospital again next week when Ali Willis underwent surgery. Clasping her arms tightly across her chest, she paced the small confines of the kitchen.

At the hospital she could keep her contact with him strictly professional. She'd make sure that there wouldn't be any moments alone with him. Not in the elevator or her office or anywhere else. If they weren't alone together, he couldn't set her pulse to racing with his nearness or the tender look in his eyes.

She stopped pacing and leaned on the counter. That was all she had to do. She would avoid any time alone with him.

Grabbing up her glass, she pressed it against the ice dispenser on the fridge and filled the tumbler to the brim. Closing her eyes, she pressed the chilled container to her temple and sighed.

The practical side of her mind quickly pointed out the obvious flaw in her plan. They hadn't been alone together out on the veranda just moments ago and he'd still managed to send her into a tailspin.

The cool glass against her face reminded her of his description of the cool morning air up in the hills. It was so easy to visualize walking hand in hand with him to the perfect spot to watch the dawn.

Her eyes flew open. What was she doing daydreaming about a date with the man?

She disliked everything he stood for. He and

his newspaper were exploiting Ali's tragic story for material gain. The very idea made her sick to her stomach. His job was to snoop while there were things in her past she wanted to keep buried. Her gut instinct told her that if Rob ever suspected she was hiding something, he would go after it like Conan after a buried bone and dig up whatever dirt he could find in the process.

Exposing Pamela to the pain Rob might uncover was something Nora simply wouldn't allow.

Determined to remain resolute and unaffected by Rob's presence, Nora left the kitchen and returned to the porch. Everyone was laughing at something Rob had said. She smiled as she joined the group and took a sip of her tea.

In the sudden quiet that settled over the gathering, Nora felt his eyes on her. She was proud that she managed to swallow her drink without choking.

"Has there been any word about John and Whitney Harpswell?" Pamela asked.

Olga shook her head. "Nothing."

Rob tilted his head. "Harpswell? Aren't they the newlywed soldiers who are missing from their camp in the Middle East?"

Olga nodded. She reached over and covered

Caitlin's hand with her own. "We are praying for them constantly."

"Are they relatives of yours?" Rob asked.

Olga smiled sadly. "No, although Whitney's brother lives here. After my husband, Anna's father, was killed in Afghanistan and we came to this country, God showed me a way to heal my own grief by helping others. It is through Him that true healing comes to us although it seems at times that life is so unfair."

"It does seem that way," Caitlin agreed. "My sister and her husband were killed not long ago, and I became the guardian of their twin daughters, Amanda and Josie."

"They are adorable girls," Pamela added.

Olga looked at Rob. "At the grief counseling center we have a program called Adopt-a-Soldier for the children. It's a wonderful way for them to feel like they are helping others. The twins adopted Whitney and John Harpswell."

Caitlin looked down at her hands. "The girls chose them because they reminded them a little bit of their mother and father. They have been exchanging e-mails with the couple, with my help of course because the girls are only kindergartners. Now, John and Whitney are missing in action. The girls are praying so hard for their safe return. I'm worried about what another loss will do to them."

"The girls are strong, and you are strong, too," Olga stated firmly. Caitlin looked at her and nodded.

Rob said. "I know the area well. The terrain is really rugged. The desert marches right up to the mountains there. It would be easy to be cut off from camp the way the fighting has been moving back and forth in the area."

"Were you stationed there?" Nora asked. It was frightening to picture him in the thick of battle half the world away.

"I was at the camp a few times. The majority of my time was spent with the local tribesmen. They are mostly nomadic herdsmen."

He gave her a lopsided grin. "A few of them do a little gunrunning and smuggling on the side. My job was to infiltrate enemy territory and spot potential strike targets. To move undetected by the enemy in that area can be done, but it's easier if you have help."

"I pray that someone is there to help John and Whitney," Olga added fervently.

"Amen," he said softly and bowed his head.

A shiver skittered down Nora's spine at the reverent timber of his voice. He made no secret of his belief but wore it openly. How did he reconcile the horror of war with his vision of a loving God? How did he hold on to his faith? She longed to ask him that question, but before she could, she heard a phone inside the building begin to ring.

"That's my cue to get back to work," Laura said. Setting her glass on the tray, she jumped to her feet and hurried away.

Anna rose and stretched her hand out to Rob. "I have a number of calls I need to make myself. Please let me know if you have any other questions, Mr. Dale."

He shook her hand. "I'll do that."

Turning to Nora, Anna said, "Thank you again for your help in getting the drugs we need. You are a true blessing."

"I do what I can."

"As do we all." Anna looked at Caitlin. "Do you have the e-mail address for the company that wanted to donate shoes?"

"I have their card on my desk." The two women walked into the building.

Olga rose as well and moved to stand in front of Nora. Reaching out, she grasped Nora's hand. "Major Jackson's wife came to the center this morning. She wanted me to be sure and thank you for all you did for her husband."

"It wasn't enough or he wouldn't have died."

"Don't be so hard on yourself, dear. Our Lord decides when we are called home and it was Major Jackson's time."

Nora raised her chin and shook her head. "I don't believe that."

Olga patted her hand. "Not now perhaps, but I have faith that you will in time."

Turning to Pamela, Olga said, "You wanted to talk to me about the library book exchange we have planned, didn't you?"

"I did, if you have a few minutes." Pamela picked up the tray with the empty glasses.

"I do, and inside I have a sketch of the area we'd like to use. Please excuse us." Olga nodded to Rob and Nora and led the way into the house, holding open the door for Pamela.

Suddenly, Nora found herself alone with Rob. It was exactly what she wanted to avoid.

So why am I still standing here?

Rob saw the uncertainty in Nora's eyes and knew just how she felt. This was unfamiliar emotional territory. As a scout for the army he knew how to read the land, how to find the high ground, how to use the cover of hills and gullies to his advantage. None of that knowledge helped him now.

Why had he made such a fool of himself

talking about picnics at dawn? The thought that she might have been laughing at him glued his usually glib tongue to the roof of his mouth like a spoonful of peanut butter would.

The silence stretched between them. At last, she said, "Don't let me keep you if you have somewhere to go, Mr. Dale."

"I'm free until dinner. I was hoping that we had known each other long enough for you to call me Rob."

Crossing her arms over her chest, she stared at the ground. "Are you finished with your story on Children of the Day, Rob?"

He loved the breathless way she said his name and wished she would say it again.

"Not quite. I have a few more angles to check into."

Wariness appeared in her eyes. "Angles? What kind of angles? I would think that the organization is very straightforward. They do wonderful and much-needed work."

The indignation in her tone made him smile. Was she always so quick to defend those she considered friends? Would she ever see him in that light?

He settled his hip on the porch's wide rail. "Every story has layers, Nora. Nothing is quite as simple as it seems. I'm sure it's the same for the patients you see. None of them is simply a heart needing repair."

Tilting her head slightly, she said, "That's true. Every patient is unique. Some of them come with complex sets of problems."

"Like Major Jackson?"

She sighed deeply. "Yes. His problems were more complex than most."

"The other morning you said *if* Cara Dempsey had died you still wouldn't have had the luxury of allowing your feelings to interfere with your work. You were actually talking about Major Jackson, weren't you? He was the one who died."

"Yes, but it doesn't matter."

He wanted to offer her comfort and reassurance. "It matters, but I understand what you are saying. It comes with the territory, doesn't it? Sometimes we have to go on no matter what. Do you ever feel like throwing back your head and howling at God in anger for putting you in that position?"

A small smile tugged at the corner of her mouth. "I don't believe in God, but sometimes I rage at the injustices I see."

"Who are you raging at?"

She shrugged. "Life. The universe."

"That is God," he said gently.

Meeting his gaze with a degree of speculation, she asked, "What about you? Do you ever rage at Him?"

"I have a few times in my life."

"Weren't you afraid that lightning would strike you down?"

He knew she was trying to sound sarcastic, but he could see an interest that she couldn't disguise. She was curious about his relationship with God, and that was fine by him.

"As I recall, I was more worried about the next incoming mortar round."

Her smile faded. "Was it terrible to be in the war?"

How to answer that? How could someone who hadn't been there comprehend what it was like? He searched for the words to explain it but couldn't find them.

"I understand if you'd rather not talk about it." The gentleness of her words surprised and touched him.

"Thanks. It wasn't always bad, but today is far too nice a day to talk about the times that were bad."

She stepped up to the railing and raised her face to the breeze. "Yes, it's too beautiful out today to dwell in the dark places of our past."

What kind of dark places haunted her eyes and filled them with sadness? He wanted to ask, but he knew it was too soon for that. He sensed that the fragile connection they had at this minute could all too easily be lost.

"Did I sound like a total moron telling Olga to take her Pastor Fields on a breakfast hike for her first date?"

She braced her hands on the rail and ducked her face. He knew she was smiling. He leaned forward and was rewarded with a glimpse of her mirth.

She sent him a sidelong glance. "Not a total moron," she admitted. "But did you notice the cowboy boots she had on? I can't see her hiking far in those."

"What about you? Do you like hikes and strawberry jam?" He waited with bated breath for her answer.

The laughter left her eyes as she stared at him. Her lips parted, but she didn't speak. Instead she suddenly drew back, and he felt the bitter pang of defeat. The tenuous thread between them had been broken.

She looked toward the house. "If you will excuse me, I have to see what's keeping Pamela. We have another appointment and I don't want to be late."

"Of course."

As he watched her hurry inside, he balled his

fingers into a fist and tapped the railing in frustration. For a second, they had shared a closeness that he wasn't ready to abandon.

Which didn't make sense. He wouldn't be in town long enough to pursue a relationship with Nora, but illogical as it seemed, that was exactly what he wanted to do.

His musing on the subject was cut short by the ring of his cell phone. He pulled it from his hip pocket and frowned when he saw the number on the display. It was his private investigator. He glanced at the door where Nora had gone inside. A stab of guilt cut through him. Did he really want to hear about Nora's past from someone other than her?

The memory of his boss telling him he hadn't done a thorough job on his last assignment was as clear as the persistent beeping of his phone. He flipped it open and walked to the far end of the veranda. "Dale here."

"Rob, this is Murray. I got that information you wanted."

"Okay, go ahead."

"There isn't much to tell. Children of the Day was started by a woman named Anna Terenkov about five years ago. Her mother emigrated from Russia about a year after her husband was killed in Afghanistan. It looks like

Anna was about thirteen at the time. The mother is some kind of counselor."

"She's a grief counselor at a church here," Rob supplied.

"Right. Anyway, the charity looks to be on the up-and-up from this end. I can try making a few calls to my overseas contacts, but I don't know anyone operating in the same areas," Murray admitted.

"The paper has a reporter near one of the places they have a refugee camp. I could ask him to check into it." Rob didn't like the idea of asking Carter for help, but if that was his only option, he'd use it.

"Are you talking about the guy who got your assignment?"

"Carter is covering my area temporarily."

"That's not the way I heard it, but you would know." Murray's tone clearly said he wasn't convinced.

"Anything on Dr. Blake?"

"Not much. She was born in Boston. She's from a working-class family."

Rob cut in impatiently. "I know all that. Skip to when she got married unless you have something unusual before then."

"Nope, she seems squeaky clean. Nothing but a traffic ticket when she was in college. She married into money. Bernard Blake was the owner and CEO of Hannor Pharmaceuticals."

"Hannor. That name rings a bell." Rob searched his memory but couldn't put his finger on why it was familiar.

"I'm not surprised. They had a stake in everything from aspirin to the latest heart drugs."

"No, it's not that. It'll come to me. What was his story?"

"His first wife died in a car accident when their daughter—"

"Pamela." Rob supplied the name with another twinge of guilt.

"That's it. The girl was only three at the time. Everyone I talked to said they were surprised when he married a woman half his age because he'd been a single father for twelve years. After he remarried, he and his new wife hit the social scene in Washington, DC, big time. People said he liked to show her off."

"I've met her and I can't blame him."

"People said it was his thing, not hers. She could dress the part but never really fit in. Too obsessed with her work."

That jived with the Nora he knew. "Anything else?"

"Blake and his company were in the news a few times with big charity donations. The bulk of it was overseas to really poor countries. Other than that, there isn't much. The company looked to be in some financial trouble about two years before he died, but he turned it around nicely. He died six years ago in some kind of skiing accident in the Swiss Alps."

"Anything funny about that?"

"Funny as in getting an old husband out of the way so the young wife could enjoy his money? Not that I can tell. The wife and daughter were here in the States at the time. The only odd thing is that she broke up the company and sold it off after he died."

"So she made a tidy profit there." Rob considered if that was something he needed—or wanted—to look into further.

"Not really." Murray sounded puzzled. "She actually took a loss on most of it. The lady might be a good surgeon, but she doesn't have a head for business."

Rob relaxed for the first time since the call started. He hadn't uncovered anything shady in Nora's past. Her husband's death was the reason for the lost and hurt look he saw in her eyes. It made sense if she were still grieving for him.

"Do you want me to keep digging?" Murray asked.

"Into Nora Blake? No, but dig a little deeper into Hannor Pharmaceuticals. I can't think why that name sticks in my head."

"You're paying the bills. I'll call you if I find anything."

Rob closed the phone just as Nora and Pamela came out of the building. Pamela waved, but Nora didn't look in his direction and he was relieved. He was afraid his guilt at prying into her past might be written all over his face.

Nora walked briskly down the steps of Children of the Day with Pamela at her heels. She wanted to put as much distance between herself and Rob as possible. The man possessed an uncanny ability to unnerve her.

"Nora, slow down. What's the hurry?"

"I want to see if my hairdresser can work me in today. This is the only day I have free this week and I need a haircut."

"Oh, that's a good idea. I'll go with you."

As they turned the corner at Veteran's Boulevard and Nora was sure she was out of Rob's sight, she slowed her pace. Now she could take a deep breath and relax.

The boulevard was the main street in Prairie Springs. In one direction it led to a bridge just outside the main gates of Fort Bonnell. In the other direction, it ran through the bustling two-mile-long business district of the community that thrived outside one of the country's largest military bases.

The town's sense of pride and patriotism was evident in the Texas and American flags displayed everywhere from storefronts to private homes.

"You don't have to keep me company." Nora gave her stepdaughter what she hoped was a normal smile.

"I don't mind. I can help you pick out a better hairstyle."

Giving Pamela a perplexed look, Nora asked, "What's wrong with this style?"

Reaching out, Pamela tugged on the hair below Nora's clip. "Nothing's wrong with it except that it isn't a style. It's a ponytail. You need something that's younger and bouncy around your face to make you look less severe."

Nora stopped. "You think I look severe?"

"A little."

Shaking her head, Nora began walking again. "This is ridiculous. Who cares what I look like?"

"But you have such pretty hair. There are women everywhere who pay large sums of money to get your gorgeous honey wheat tones.

You're always scraping it back into a roll or a clip."

"I like to be able to get my hair out of the way."

"You don't like to look friendly?"

Nora's jaw dropped. "What kind of question is that?"

"Just because you're a brilliant surgeon doesn't mean you have to go around looking like a frump."

Nora stopped again and stared in amazement at Pamela. "Now you're telling me that I'm frumpy."

"Not today. The color of that shirt looks great on you, but how many outfits do you have that aren't black or gray?"

"Lots."

"Not counting the blue and green scrubs you wear."

Taking a quick mental inventory of her closet, Nora said, "Several."

"Three."

"Three is several." Nora started walking again.

"Three is not enough."

Grabbing her stepmother's arm, Pamela turned her toward the display window of a boutique. "That outfit would look delicious on you."

The mannequin in the window wore a long

peach-colored tunic with wide, three-quarter-length sleeves over a pair of matching slacks. Nora studied it but shook her head. "It's too young for me. You should get it."

Pamela dragged her toward the store. "You make yourself sound like Olga's Russian grandmother. It is not too young for you. Humor me. Try it on and then tell me it doesn't look good on you."

Twenty minutes later, with two new outfits in a shopping bag on her arm, Nora followed Pamela out of the boutique, not quite certain how her stepdaughter had managed to talk her into buying both the pantsuit and a new dress. She had to admit that Pamela was right. Both outfits, but especially the simple red sheath dress, looked stunning on her.

What would Rob think if he saw her in it?

She tried to dismiss the idea by telling herself she didn't care what he thought of her wardrobe, but it wouldn't quite go away. Some small part of her knew he would like it.

Feeling more lighthearted than she had in months, Nora enjoyed Pamela's teasing as the two of them window-shopped their way toward the beauty parlor two blocks down the street. The little bell over the door jangled as they went in, and Nora was happy to see that her stylist was free.

"Thea, do you have time to give me a trim?"

"Dr. Blake, how nice to see you. Yes, I have time for you. Have a seat."

Pamela took the bags from Nora's hands as Nora sat in the empty chair. "She doesn't want just a trim, Ms. Thea. She wants a new style."

"Really?" Thea's face brightened. "I so glad to hear you say that. I know just what we should do."

Nora listened to the enthusiastic pair discuss her hair quality, face shape and style options with trepidation. There had been a time when she had been a bit vain about her hair. Bernard had always loved it when she wore it up. He used to say it made her look regal. She still wore it in a French twist when she wanted to present a poised front. In a way, it was part of her armor.

Armor? When had she stopped thinking of herself as a woman? Closing her eyes, she said, "All right. Cut it—but not too short."

She kept her eyes closed until Thea finished snipping, curling and brushing to her satisfaction. Turning the chair at last, Thea pulled off the plastic cape and said, "There. What do you think?"

Nora peeked cautiously, then opened her eyes wide. It was like looking at a different person.

Styled from a side part, her hair now fell to a few inches past her jaw line in a soft, feathery cascade. The bangs that were swept to one side definitely made her look younger. She turned her face first one way and then the other. "It looks…"

"It look fabulous, Thea. You are a genius! Don't you just love it, Mom?"

Nora wasn't sure. "It's going to take a little getting used to."

"It's always that way with a new style. Take our word for it, you look great."

After paying Thea and adding a generous tip, Nora gathered up her belongings. She left the shop feeling the unfamiliar swing of her hair against her neck as she moved. Glancing at her reflection in the plate glass window, she decided it wasn't a bad style. It was kind of fun. Besides, it would grow out again.

Pamela glanced at her watch. "We still have to stop at the grocery store and it's already after four. We need to get going."

"What's the hurry? I thought we might go out to dinner."

"Oh, we can't tonight."

Nora detected a tone she hadn't heard in Pamela's voice since the girl had been a teenager. Something was up.

"Why not?" Nora asked. "Surly you aren't ashamed to be seen with your frumpy step-mother now that I have a new hairdo."

"It's not that."

"Okay, what is it?"

Pamela scrunched her face as she said, "We're kind of…having company for dinner tonight."

Nora's stomach did a flip-flop. "Who's coming to dinner?"

Pamela bit her lip, then smiled with false brightness. "I invited Rob Dale."

Chapter Eight

Nora flinched when her doorbell rang a few minutes before seven o'clock that evening. She glared at her stepdaughter.

"That must be him," Pamela said cheerfully as she laid a third place at the table.

"I can't believe you invited that man to dinner." Nora slammed the lid on the pasta simmering on the back burner of the stove. As much as she wanted to be angry, a quickening sense of excitement bubbled through her veins.

Pamela came up behind her and gave her a quick hug. "Relax. The guy has been eating takeout and restaurant food for days. I felt sorry for him. All I did was offer him a home-cooked meal and a chance to get out of his motel room for an evening. Anna is feeding him tomorrow night, so it isn't like this is anything special. Now stop pouting and behave."

As Pamela headed for the door, Nora called after her. "Who is the mother in this house, anyway? It's my job to tell *you* to behave, not the other way around."

Pamela's answer was an airy wave of her hand. Nora rolled her eyes and pulled the hissing pan off the burner. It was clear that Pamela had no idea what an awkward position she had placed her stepmother in.

I can do this. I can spend the evening being polite but cool. He is Pamela's guest, not mine. With any luck, he won't stay long.

She glanced toward the living room and frowned when she heard his voice followed by Pamela's laughter. She would have to warn Pamela that the man was a consummate flirt. Pamela was normally a level-headed young woman, but Rob Dale had a way of mesmerizing a person.

Nora pressed her hands to her midsection to quell her jitters. As her palms touched the sleek fabric of her new dress, she suddenly wished she hadn't allowed Pamela to talk her into buying, let alone wearing, the bright form-fitting outfit. Of course it was too late now to change.

She chided herself for being silly. He

couldn't possibly know it was a new dress. He certainly wouldn't expect her to entertain in her scrubs.

Carrying the steaming pan to the sink, she strained the penne and transferred it to a waiting bowl.

"Is there anything I can do to help?" The sound of his voice close behind her made her jump.

"Whoa!" He grabbed the bowl of pasta as it skittered out of her grip to the edge of the counter.

She whirled around to find him only inches away. "You startled me."

"Sorry." His smile didn't look the least bit apologetic.

"That's quite all right." She hoped she didn't sound as breathless as she felt.

She sidestepped him, but not before she noticed how his cobalt blue crewnecked shirt outlined the athletic muscles of his chest. The color made his eyes seem even brighter. Or maybe it was just the humor that lurked in them.

He tilted his head slightly. "You've done something different with your hair."

She raked her fingers through her bangs and brushed them back self-consciously. "I got a trim today, that's all."

"I like it. The shorter style really suits you."

His flattery sent heat rushing to her cheeks. She struggled to replace her giddiness with cool politeness. "Thank you. Dinner is almost ready. Please have a seat. Where is Pamela?"

"She said she needed to powder her nose. This smells great. It was really nice of your stepdaughter to invite me. I hope I'm not putting you out."

"Of course not." It wasn't cooking an extra serving that was difficult, it was keeping her wits about her when he was so close.

Rob looked around. "Where's the barbarian?"

Relieved to be free of Rob's close scrutiny, Nora headed to the table and began straightening the silverware. "He's outside in the backyard."

"He hasn't been banished on my account, has he?"

"Conan doesn't have the best manners at mealtime. I hope you like Italian cooking," she said in a rush to cover her nervousness.

"I do."

"Then you'll love Nora's chicken and pasta in her special creamy pesto sauce," Pamela said as she came strolling in. Nora relaxed a fraction.

Rob chuckled. "That's almost a tongue twister. It's a good thing you aren't cooking it. Pamela's chicken and pasta in special creamy pesto sauce would be tricky to say six times."

Pamela dissolved into a fit of giggles as Rob grinned at her. Nora stared at the two of them laughing together like they had known each other for years instead of hours. Abruptly, she turned away.

It wasn't jealously that made the sight painful. It was knowing that Rob Dale had the power to hurt Pamela as easily as he amused her. Nora wouldn't allow herself to forget that fact—no matter how much she found herself wishing she could.

Throughout dinner, Rob remained acutely aware of the woman seated across from him. Nora barely touched her food. She toyed with her salad and then with a small portion of chicken while he managed a second hearty helping. The food was good, but it couldn't sidetrack him from the question that had been plaguing him since he arrived. Why did Nora seem so uncomfortable? Was it just because he was here, or did she have something else on her mind?

Even distracted, she managed to look especially lovely. Her red dress accentuated her slender figure and put color in her cheeks. The soft way her hair curved around her face made her eyes seem bigger and more luminous. She certainly didn't look like the Dr. Ice Princess he had met that first day.

Had it only been a week ago? It didn't seem possible that he had become so drawn to a woman in such a short time. If only he could find a way to break through the barrier she used to keep him at arm's length. More than anything, he found himself wanting to know her better, to see where these budding feelings would take them both.

"Are you enjoying your time in Prairie Springs, Rob?" Pamela asked. Nora's stepdaughter had turned out to be an engaging woman with a quick wit and a ready laugh. To his amusement, he also found her to be a determined interviewer.

"It's a little quiet for my tastes. It reminds me of my hometown. The sidewalks get rolled up in Dodge City at sundown, just like here."

"So you prefer the big city?" Pamela lifted her glass and took a sip of water.

"I prefer to go where the news is. What about you? Do you miss the excitement of Washington, DC? It must have been hard to move to a small Texas town after growing up in the capital."

Looking taken aback, Pamela asked, "How did you know I grew up in DC?"

"I have my sources."

Nora's fork clattered to her plate. Her eyes widened, then her gaze slide away from his. He had pricked a nerve, but which one?

Pamela dismissed him with a wave of her hand. "Oh, you looked me up on Google, didn't you. I'm flattered, but I'm sure you didn't find much. I'm not exactly newsworthy. Now, Nora, on the other hand, has published dozens of articles and made the news a number of times for her work with children."

"Rob isn't interested in hearing about us. His story is Children of the Day. Isn't that right?"

Did he detect a challenge in Nora's eyes. "That was my assignment to begin with, but a good reporter is always on the lookout for the next big scoop."

Pamela laughed. "The only big scoop in Prairie Springs is the triple-decker ice-cream cone at the Creamery downtown."

"Speaking of ice cream, can I get you some dessert?" Nora rose and picked up his empty plate.

"No, thank you. I'm stuffed. The chicken was delicious."

She inclined her head ever so slightly. "I'm glad you liked it."

"It was the best I've had in a long time. You'll have to give me the recipe." There was a hint of a blush in her cheeks again and he smiled. Was she so unused to compliments?

"Do you like to cook?" Pamela asked.

He tore his gaze away from Nora's face. "I try my hand at it when I'm at home."

"And where is home?" Pamela inquired. "Still Dodge City?"

Nora interrupted. "We don't need to keep Rob here with our chitchat. I'm sure he has things he needs to do."

"I don't have anywhere else to be. I'm free for the whole evening."

Nora's smile in response to his comment appeared stilted, but she hid her chagrin well. Turning her back on him, she carried the empty plates into the kitchen.

"Home at present," he said, "is a tiny apartment in Washington, DC."

Pamela's eyes lit up. "Oh, what part?"

"Somerset."

Clapping her hands together, Pamela said, "We used to live in Brookdale. Is Mario's Pizza Palace still on the corner across from the park?"

He nodded. "It is."

"My dad used to take us there. Remember, Nora?"

"I remember." She came back to the table and gathered up the water glasses. "He loved their pepperoni. He always said it was the best pizza in or out of the country."

"Then he traveled a lot?" Rob posed the question he already knew the answer to. Nora kept her gaze down.

"When I was little I thought he traveled too much," Pamela said sadly. "After he married Nora, he stayed home more and I liked that, but then—"

"I'm sure Rob isn't interested in our ancient history, Pamela," Nora interjected.

"Of course." Pamela smiled at Rob. "I'm sorry. Would you like a tour of the house? My father collected some very nice artifacts from around the world, and I've kept a few of his favorite pieces. After that I'll show you Nora's studio downstairs. You'll be amazed by her talent."

"No!" Nora objected so quickly that both he and Pamela looked at her in astonishment.

"Forgive me." Nora picked up several more dishes. "It's just such a mess down there. Don't take him downstairs, but you really should show him your father's collection of Chinese carvings. I'm sure he'd rather see that than my crewel-work. I'll make some coffee for us and we can have it in the den."

"All right." Pamela gave her mother a

puzzled look but led the way out of the kitchen. Rob followed, but he had very little interest in seeing an art collection. What he wanted was to find out why Nora didn't want him to see her studio.

As he followed Pamela into the large wood-paneled den adjacent to the living room, Rob took stock of Nora's home. It was certainly nice but by no means lavish. The furniture was solid, not trendy. It supported Murray's assertion that she hadn't made a lot of money after her husband's death.

As he looked over Bernard Blake's collection of delicate and intricately carved panels and pottery, he admitted silently that the man had an eye for beauty. Rob glanced up at Pamela. "This is impressive, but at the risk of sounding stupid, can I ask a question?"

"Certainly."

"What kind of torturous work does Nora do in the cellar?"

"Torturous?" The look she gave him questioned his sanity.

"She said I wouldn't want to look at her cruel work."

Pamela laughed out loud. "Crewel. C-r-e-w-e-l. It's a type of needlework."

He pressed a hand to his chest. "That's a

relief. I was worried. I though the doctor was hiding a diabolical laboratory in the cellar."

She patted his arm. "You're so funny."

"I try. So tell me about your father. I know he was the CEO of Hannor Pharmaceuticals."

"How did you know that? No, don't tell me. You have your sources."

"That's right." He admitted with a small pang of guilt.

"My dad was a great guy in so many ways. I'm really proud of his legacy. Oh, not these artifacts, but the way he helped people. His company made major discoveries in the area of heart disease research, but even more than that— he was a great humanitarian. His company donated more drugs to third world countries than his next two biggest competitors combined."

"That is something to be proud of. Nora certainly seems intent on following his lead with her work for Children of the Day."

"She does a lot more than help Children of the Day. When Mercy Medical Center halted funding for the new PICU, Nora donated a substantial sum to get the project underway again."

"Really?" Rob filed the fact away for future reference. "No one mentioned that. In fact, she the donation was made anonymously."

ora's lifestyle didn't suggest that she had a

quarter million dollars lying around waiting to be given away. Not that he was any judge of how the wealthy lived. His family had lived paycheck to paycheck when he was growing up. No doubt a cardiac surgeon pulled in a tidy salary—for sure more than a reporter.

Pamela bit her lip and looked as if she had said too much. "Please don't mention that I told you about it. She would hate it if that got out."

"Why is that?"

"Because she's a very private person." Forcing a smile, she continued, "Nor was my father one to brag. However, you mustn't think he cared only about his work. After my mother died, he raised me alone and we were best buddies. He always had time for my dance recitals and school plays. He never acted like a big shot. He was just, Dad."

"Did that change when he married Nora?"

She cocked her head to the side. "Why, Rob, I believe I see the nosy reporter rearing his curious head."

"Sorry. Force of habit. You don't have to tell me anything. We can talk about sixteenth-century jade dragons or the weather."

She regarded him silently for a moment. "No, I don't often get a chance to talk about my dad. When he died, Nora had a very difficult time, and I know she doesn't like to discuss it."

"I don't want you to do anything that will upset her."

"Nor do I, but it was my life, too, and I like to share my memories. Things changed a little after they were married. Dad spent more time socializing, but you know how Washington is. Big money is courted on a very grand scale there. I'm sure you've seen that for yourself."

"Occasionally. That must have been hard on you, seeing him with a new wife."

"I was fifteen and a royal pain at that stage of my life. The truth of the matter is that I *was* jealous at first, but once I saw how warm and genuine Nora was, I knew Dad had made the right decision. She was the best big sister-girl-friend-mother that any spoiled brat could hope to find."

"I can't see you as a spoiled brat."

"Oh, believe me, I was. If this is off the record, I'll tell you about the time I got four nannies in a row to quit their first week on the job.

"I'd love to hear the story, but the truth is, nothing is ever really off the record."

She laid a finger against her lips and tapped it several times. "Hmm. I think I'll take a chance and trust you. It involved my friend Greg and his pet rats."

With Pamela and Rob out of sight, Nora sagged against the kitchen counter and crossed her arms over her middle. Pamela would quiz her later about her overreaction, but by then Nora would have a plausible excuse and her nerves wouldn't be stretched to the breaking point the way they had been all through dinner.

She drew a deep, calming breath. It wasn't as if she had done anything wrong. She had a right to her privacy. Her studio was her sanctuary, her escape from the madness and pressures of her work. She wasn't ashamed of it, she just didn't want *him* there.

The sound of Rob's deep laughter and Pamela's giggle reached Nora from the other end of the house. The thought that it might not be wise to leave the two of them alone spurred her into action.

Nora opened the fridge, then pulled out a bag of gourmet coffee. As she spooned the grounds into the maker, the pungent aroma helped to calm her jitters. While the coffee dripped its way into the pot, she brought out her seldom-used silver service. She quickly filled the sugar bowl and cream pitcher. A few minutes later she transferred the piping hot brew into the ornate urn.

Tray in hand, she left the safety of the kitchen and entered the den. Rob, standing beside the display case, hurried across the room. "Let me get that for you."

His hands brushed hers as he took hold of the heavy tray. A fission of electricity seemed to arch between them. She met his gaze and couldn't look away.

His usually merry eyes darkened with emotion and seemed to draw her in with a tenderness she had never experienced. She held her breath, afraid to break the cocoon of warmth that surrounded them.

Pamela cleared her throat. "I'll pour."

Nora let loose of the tray and rubbed her palms on the sides of her dress. Rob, for once seemingly at a loss for words, carried the platter to the low table in front of the burgundy leather love seat and pair of wing-backed leather chairs that faced the fireplace.

Nora sat on the edge of one chair and Rob sat in the other one. Pamela poured the coffee into the three gold-rimmed, delicate china cups. The silence grew. Nora racked her brain for something to say that wouldn't sound inane but couldn't come up with anything. She could feel his eyes on her. She licked her suddenly dry lips.

Pamela handed a cup and saucer to Nora and then one to Rob. He nodded his thanks and took a quick sip. He nodded again. "This is good. It beats the stuff they serve at the Prairie Springs Inn. I mean, the coffee there is okay, but this is…better. The service is good there. I've stayed at a lot worse places…and…at some better ones."

He smiled and took another sip.

Pamela sat back on the love seat with a small smile just curving the corner of her lips. "How interesting."

Nora caught her stepdaughter's knowing look and wanted to shake her. Calling up the memory of the cool reserve and polite small talk that had surrounded her among Bernard's friends, she looked at Rob and said, "Where do you go after you leave Prairie Springs?"

"Hopefully, back to the Middle East." His eagerness to return was evident.

"Back to war?" A chill raised goose flesh on Nora's arms. She tried to tell herself that she would feel concern for anyone going into harm's way.

"Back to covering the war and other stories there. After serving twelve years in that part of the Middle East, it's almost like my backyard. I know the people there. I respect them, and they respect me."

"What is keeping you from going back?" Nora asked, intrigued in spite of herself.

"I messed up on my last assignment. Another reporter did a better job. My paper sent him to take my place for the next month. If he does a good job he could earn a permanent assignment, but covering in-depth stories there requires contacts. I have them in the area, he doesn't. So I still have a shot at getting back there."

"I would have thought you had seen enough of war after your time in the army." Nora knew she sounded disapproving.

"There were times when I thought that, too, but then I'd meet some kid from Indiana who was using his army pay to buy books and pencils for a village school with only ten kids who'd never seen a book in their lives. Then there was this coffee merchant and his wife who smuggled arms to the freedom fighters in the hills at the risk of their own lives.

"The struggle for liberty has so many faces that we never see in the sound bites on the six o'clock news. I wanted to tell those stories."

Intrigued with this new facet of the man, Nora

asked, "Do you believe what you write will make a difference in how people see the conflict?"

"I don't write stories to try and change people's perceptions. I write to shine a light on a subject or a person that may have otherwise gone unnoticed, because everything and everyone is important.

"That GI from the Midwest isn't a particularly important fellow except to his folks and maybe a girlfriend. I doubt he's going to become our next president. Well, who knows? Maybe he will someday, but what he did was important in a life-changing way to ten school-kids who don't even speak his language."

"I think your profession sounds like a very noble one," Pamela said.

"It can be. I try to live my life with God's work in mind, but Nora thinks I'm exploiting little Ali by writing his story." He was grinning when he said it, obviously trying to bait her.

"I don't think you are exploiting the boy. I think your paper is exploiting his suffering for gain." She touched the locket at her neck but put her hand down when she realized he was watching her.

Rob held his hands palm up as if balancing her words. "There isn't much difference, but I can see your point."

She inclined her head ever so slightly. "Thank you."

"My paper is in business to make money, that's a hard fact of life that I can't change, but I'd like to point out the good we do. Thousands upon thousands of people will learn about Children of the Day from what I write."

"That's certainly true," she admitted, "but what angle will you use?"

"Angle?"

"You said you were checking all the angles. Will your readers learn about the difficult but important work being done by Anna and a dedicated few, or will they read that a nonprofit charity helped a three-star general pull strings to get his grandson into this country for heart surgery?"

Rob raised his eyebrows and cocked his head to one side. "Both stories are true."

Clearly appalled, Pamela said, "You aren't going to print that Anna or anyone at Children of the Day did something unethical, are you?"

"I would if that were the case."

"Of course they didn't do anything wrong. Why would you think that?" Pamela's indignation was an echo of Nora's feelings on the subject.

"He would think it because it would make a *sensational* story," Nora said with a pointed look in his direction.

"It would have been a *great* story if a former U.S. Army general had misused his position. I'm happy to say that wasn't the case. The general called in a few favors to get his grandson escorted here by an army nurse, but she was on her way here anyway, so that wasn't out of line. He's paying all the bills for the boy's medical care so it's not like charity funds were misused. Children of the Day merely assisted with expediting the needed paperwork because the boy's mother worked for the organization overseas. I didn't find anything questionable in that help."

"I'm sure you've learned how much good Children of the Day has done. In spite of all that, you would have printed a story that cast them in a poor light, anyway?" Nora asked.

"I've said before that I believe God puts me where I'm needed most. If He had wanted me to reveal corruption disguised as charity, then that is what I would have found. If He wants me to reveal the true charity of the spirit that exists here, then that is what I will do."

Nora allowed herself to relax. "So you do believe in the good that is being done here?"

"I haven't seen anything to suggest otherwise. Have you?"

"No," Nora declared, happy that she could

answer with conviction. "I made sure that Children of the Day was on the level before I offered them my services."

"That's what I've found so far."

"Does that mean you'll be leaving soon?" Pamela asked.

A chill settled over Nora. On a deep level, Nora knew things would never be the same once he was gone. He had awakened something inside her that she had thought was long dead.

He nodded but didn't take his eyes off Nora. "After Ali's surgery, yes. Although, I must admit I like the country around here. I wouldn't mind coming back and spending some vacation time here."

Pamela looked hopeful. "Perhaps you could ask for another assignment in the area."

"A reporter doesn't often get to choose his assignments."

"I imagine not. This one must seem rather tame after the dangers of a war zone," Nora suggested.

"I didn't choose this one, that's true, but a mark of a good reporter is that he does an impartial job no matter how he feels about his subject matter."

Pamela nodded in understanding. "So you can't let your personal feelings interfere with your work. I think Nora has mentioned that about her work, too."

"I made that mistake recently and it cost me," he said with a wry smile.

"Everyone makes mistakes now and then," Nora said, knowing she had made her share.

"That's true," he admitted. "We're only human, but the smart thing is to learn from our mistakes."

Nora felt Rob's gaze on her and looked into his intense blue eyes. He said, "I'm trying not to let personal feelings interfere with my work here, although I'm finding that much harder than I expected."

He was talking about her. He had personal feelings for her. Nora couldn't decide if the idea pleased her or frightened her witless. In that moment, she realized she had been fighting a losing battle from the first moment he walked into her life.

She liked him. She liked him far more than she should. Against every ounce of better judgment that she possessed, she knew that seeing more of Rob Dale was exactly what she wanted to do.

Chapter Nine

The next day, Rob interviewed several more volunteers who worked regularly with Children of the Day. They all said pretty much the same thing. The charity did desperately needed work in war-torn countries around the world. Anna Terenkov might be the founder, but she was inspiring dozens of men and women to take up the cause with her.

Many of those who gave of their time were civilians, but a large number were servicemen and women who wanted to help in any way they could. The fact didn't surprise Rob. During his time in the service, he had seen the generous nature of American military personnel numerous times.

His dinner with Anna and her mother turned out to be a pleasant enough evening. The Tex-

Mex food was a little too hot for his taste, but there was plenty of it, and the women, especially Olga, provided lively conversation. While he gathered a little more insight into Anna and her organization, he knew he hadn't uncovered anything new.

Now, as he sat against the headboard of his bed at the inn and typed his notes into his computer, he knew without a doubt that his piece, while touching and filled with stories about the good individuals could do, was also bland. It wasn't the story that would wow his boss or earn back the assignment Rob wanted.

Shutting the lid of his laptop, he sat up on the edge of the bed and raked his fingers through his hair. He couldn't work tonight. His heart wasn't in it. Maybe what he needed was some fresh air to stimulate his brain. He rose and walked to the window of his second-story room at the Prairie Inn that looked out on the town square.

The street below was quiet now; the shops were closed. The street lamps made small lonely islands of light in the darkness. At the intersection just up the road, a traffic signal blinked a repeated yellow warning. Proceed with caution.

It was a sign he should heed, only his heart

was speeding ahead and he was pretty sure it was steering him into trouble.

Picking up his keys, he shoved them in the pocket of his pants and let himself out of his room. A young couple walked past as he opened his door. The man had a sleeping toddler draped over his shoulder and the young woman was looking at both of them with eyes overflowing with love.

As he watched them pass, Rob knew a moment of jealousy. Would a woman who loved him ever walk at his side? Would he ever carry his own sleeping child? The questions had never seemed so important before.

After doing a few quick stretches in the motel parking lot, he broke into a jog and headed toward the quiet downtown area. Before long his feet fell into an easy, familiar cadence and he let his mind wander. It wasn't the story that had him itching to get out of his room and run through the empty streets. It was thoughts of Nora. He longed to see her again.

Until he'd sat across the table from her he'd rarely thought about settling down, about coming home to the same woman every day. He had four brothers, all with big families to assuage his parents' need for grandchildren. Rob had always used his army career as an excuse when his siblings or parents started pressuring him about settling down. It was true, but the real reason was that he'd never met a woman like Nora.

Was she at home tonight? Or was she at the hospital mending someone's broken heart with her capable hands and gritty determination? The more he learned about the subject of pediatric cardiac surgery, the more he was awed by what she did.

That she also chose to work at Fort Bonnell's hospital proved she cared about the military men and women stationed here. She seemed almost too good to be true, except that she didn't share his faith.

What had happened to make her turn away from God's love? He wanted to know the answer. His faith was as important to him as the air he breathed. He could only imagine how empty life must be for someone who didn't believe in God's salvation. He wanted to help Nora find her way back. He wanted to hold her hand and watch the sun come up.

Turning off the main street at the next corner, he soon found himself in a residential area. An occasional dog barked at his passing, but for the most part, the stillness of the night helped settle his restlessness.

His piece on Children of the Day was almost complete. Once Nora read his article about Ali and the charity, she might be less disapproving of his work. Perhaps then they could find some common ground and begin to explore the feelings they had for each other.

What if she didn't feel the same emotions, the same sense of rightness when they were together?

As he passed by the next house on the block he let his fingers tap the tops of white picket fence. His parents had the same kind of fence in front of their home in Dodge City. The love and happiness he had known there had shaped his entire life. He stopped to gaze at the light pouring out of the large bay window of the two-story Victorian. If he ever had a family, he would want a house like that one with an inviting front yard and lots of character.

Suddenly, the light snapped off. He stood, drawing in deep breathes of the cool night air and staring at the home's dark facade.

He took a step back. What on earth was he thinking? He and Nora didn't have a relationship or any hope of a relationship. Dr. Nora Blake was way out of his league. Besides, he wasn't a picket fence type of guy. It was okay for his parents and his brothers, but he had always needed more adventure.

Besides, he'd be gone soon, back to reporting from inside a war zone if he got his wish. That was what he wanted, wasn't it?

Of course it was. Turning around, he started jogging back to the motel, but the peace of the night was gone.

Once inside his room again, he plopped on the bed and picked up the remote. Pointing it at the TV, he switched it on. A commercial was playing for a local Italian restaurant. It looked like a decent place. With another week of eating out looming in his future, he decided he might have to try it. He scribbled the name and address on the notepad by the phone.

Nora's Italian cooking had certainly been to his liking, but then almost everything about Nora seemed to be to his liking.

Giving himself a mental shake, he tried to dismiss her from his mind. He wouldn't see her again until Ali checked into the hospital for his surgery, and that was a good thing. Time away from her was exactly what he needed.

Except it wasn't what he wanted.

He crossed out the restaurant name on his notepad. He didn't need to be reminded of her when he was eating alone, either. He'd ask around and get some recommendations for places to eat. In west Texas it should be easy to find a place that didn't serve pasta and pesto sauce. On the other hand, it might be hard to find a place that didn't have jalapenos in every other dish.

He smiled as he wondered if Olga had decided where she wanted Pastor Fields to take her on their date. He'd give a day's pay to be a fly on the wall for that. During Rob's brief meeting with the pastor that morning, he'd found himself wondering exactly what the lively Russian lady saw in the man. To Rob's way of thinking, the minister was far too reserved for the gregarious and lovable woman.

Still, only God knew the ways of the heart. Perhaps the two were made for each other.

Rob clicked between the major news channels to catch the latest headline and finally switched the television off. He glanced at his watch. It was almost midnight. That would make it early morning in where Carter was in the Middle East.

Picking up his computer, he sat back against the headboard and typed in the e-mail address he'd gotten from the paper's Web site. He sent a brief note asking the reporter to check into Children of the Day's refugee camp in the area. Rob knew that not all supplies and funds raised for charity actually found their way to the needy. Often a hefty percentage found its way into the pockets of unscrupulous managers, greedy middlemen or criminal elements at both ends of the operations.

He had no idea how soon Carter might reply, but Rob decided to wait up. He was rewarded with the ding of incoming mail a half hour later. Scanning the note, he saw Carter was willing and eager to give Rob a hand with the investigation. The unwritten part of the message was that Carter would be able to ask Rob to reciprocate in the future.

The last thing Rob wanted to do was to help the rookie reporter succeed at the job that should have been his.

Late the next morning, Nora left the PICU and walked toward her office. As she reached her door, it opened and she came face to face with Rob. She froze as she stared at him in surprise. Her heart skipped a beat and then sped into overdrive. She couldn't believe how happy she was to see him. "Rob, I didn't think I'd be seeing you until Ali's surgery."

He looked embarrassed and unsure of himself. She found it endearing.

"I thought I'd stop by and get those information pamphlets on what parents can expect during their child's surgery that you told me about. You know, for background stuff for my piece."

"Oh, yes, of course. Was Delia able to get them for you?" Her irrational bubble of happiness deflated. He hadn't come just to see her.

He glanced over his shoulder and let the door close. "She did, but I don't think she liked doing it for me. She made a point of saying several times that I didn't have an appointment or a child that needed surgery."

"Delia runs a very tight ship. She doesn't like things that vary from the norm. Sometimes I'm afraid to tell her I'm going to be working late. She takes it as a personal insult if she doesn't get to lock up."

"Carmen mentioned that the woman was a bit of a dragon. I thought she was exaggerating. Look, I don't mean to keep you. I'm sure you have work to do."

"Actually, I'm caught up for a change." Was she being blatantly obvious? The smart thing would be to excuse herself and hide out in her office until he was gone, but today she didn't want to hide.

Maybe it was her new hairdo that made her feel brazen. She'd gathered several compliments on it that morning. Or maybe it was because she'd been thinking about him and now that he was here, she didn't want him to leave.

He relaxed and stuck his hands in the front pockets of his jeans. "I was just on my way to the coffee shop downstairs. If you aren't busy, I'd like to buy you a cup."

She nodded, hoping she didn't look over eager. "Sure. I have a little free time."

His engaging grin reappeared. "That's great. After you." He gestured for her to proceed him.

At the elevator, they stepped on and she tapped the button for the main level. It didn't light up. She pushed it again and nothing happened.

"Do I have to worry about you in elevators?" Rob started to reach around her.

She held up her hand. "I've got it."

She pressed the disk firmly one more time. It lit up and the car began descending. Meeting Rob's eyes in the reflection of the polished metal doors, she saw the humor sparkling in them and smiled back.

He said, "I have a confession to make. The pamphlets were just an excuse to see you again."

She couldn't hide her surprise. "They were?"

"I hope you don't mind."

Although she knew it was foolish beyond measure to admit as much, she smiled shyly and said, "I'm glad you thought of it."

"You are?"

"I am." She was still smiling when the elevator doors opened. Rob had come to see her. Bubbles of delight made her almost giddy. She hadn't felt so happy in years.

Two of the surgical nurses were waiting to get on with tall foam coffee containers in their hands. Nora nodded at them. "Good morning, Traci. Hello, Emily."

Traci's eyebrows shot up. Emily looked taken aback but managed to say, "Hello, Dr. Blake."

Nora continued across the lobby into the trendy coffee shop that occupied a small room beside the hospital's gift shop. She noted with relief that the half dozen booths were empty. After giving their order at the counter, they sat down and waited for the teenage girl to bring them their drinks.

When they were alone, Rob said, "I wanted to thank you for dinner the other night. You and your stepdaughter were exceeding nice to open your home to a stranger."

"It was nothing."

"Oh, but it was something. Not everyone would do that. Especially if they feel about reporters the way that you do."

"I don't have anything against reporters in general,"

"So it's me in particular you don't like."

She stared at him, aghast. "Oh, no!"

Tilting his head, he said, "I'm kidding."

She relaxed. "Sorry. I don't get much levity in my day-to-day life here. Mostly I get one crisis after another."

"I can't imagine doing what you do."

"You could with the right training."

"No, I can't even mend my own socks let alone stitch an artery to the heart."

"Well, that's your problem." She nodded sagely.

He cocked his eyebrow. "What is?"

Shaking her head sadly, she said, "Many men suffer from sock-sewing phobia. I can recommend a good therapist."

Rob leaned forward to look at her more closely. "Nora Blake, did you just make a joke?"

"What? You thought I didn't have a sense of humor?"

Shaking his head, he said, "I should have realized that anyone who keeps a dog like Conan can't be completely devoid of the emotion."

Her eyes narrowed. "I was wrong about you, too."

"How do you mean?"

"I apologize for accusing you of trying to

exploit Ali. I believe you sincerely want to be helpful."

Relaxing, he said, "That's good, because between you and Delia, I was beginning to think I'd lost my touch."

"Don't think I've fallen for your charms just because I've revised my opinion of your work."

He leaned toward her with a grin. "Do I have charms?"

The waitress arrived with their drinks and saved Nora from having to answer. She took a quick sip of her sweet, hot concoction.

Rob sat back in the booth. "So what made you change your mind about my work?"

"After you left the other night I searched the online archives of *Liberty and Justice* for some of your articles. I was impressed with both the pieces you talked about and some of your others. You have a knack for finding the motivation behind what people do when faced with terrible circumstances."

"I like to think so."

"I do disagree with your article assessing the military's role during natural disasters overseas."

"Really. How so?"

Rob listened to Nora's opinions with interest. She had a good grasp of international politics, and that surprised him. She was always surprising him and he enjoyed it. Now that he was with her, he couldn't remember why he thought he should stay away.

She stopped talking to take a sip of her coffee. He said, "Would you allow me to repay your dinner invitation with one of my own for tomorrow night?"

He saw her hesitation and added, "For both you and Pamela, of course. I was hoping you could suggest a local restaurant that isn't quite so…Texan."

"La Primo Bistro is good if you like Mediterranean food, and it's only a few blocks from here."

"That sounds great." Anywhere sounded good if she accepted his offer. His hopes rose.

"I'll have to ask Pamela if she has any plans."

"Of course, but if she can't make it at least let me buy dinner for you."

A reticent expression crossed her face and she stared down at her coffee. "You don't have to do that."

"I know I don't have to, but I'd like to. What do you say?" He held his breath willing her to say yes.

Later that same evening, Nora glanced at the Swiss cuckoo clock on the wall of her studio when it began to chime. The miniature bird darted out of his house and chirped with wooden wings fluttering. It was eleven o'clock at night.

"Why aren't you in bed yet?" Pamela asked as she came halfway down the stairs.

"It's about time you got home," Nora said, setting her magnifying loupes aside and rubbing her eyes.

"I'm sorry I'm late. A few of us stopped at the Creamery for hot fudge sundaes after the singles meeting. I hope you weren't worried."

Turning around in her chair, Nora smiled at her stepdaughter. "Worrying is part of a mother's job."

"Which you take too seriously. I'm a big girl now. What are you working on?"

"The daughter for my newest house."

Coming to stand beside Nora, Pamela picked up the miniature doll. Only two inches tall, the girl wore a blue satin dress with delicately embroidered red roses and green leaves on the hem. "This is lovely."

"I like the way it turned out, but I think the room needs something else, I'm not sure what. I thought about a dog."

Pamela bent to peer into the interior of the two-story dollhouse. An Edwardian family, resplendent in the dignified clothing of the era, sat in a parlor on the first floor. "A dog would be good. Oh, is that a teddy bear? He's so cute."

Pamela carefully picked up the tiny stuffed toy. "You've sewn a heart on his chest."

"Not just a heart," Nora said.

Pamela looked more closely. "I see. It's two halves of a broken heart sewn together. I don't know why you didn't want Rob to see this. You are so talented and clever."

Nora shrugged and began to put her tools away. "This is just a hobby. It's not like he would be interested in it."

"Oh, I think he would."

"I saw him today," Nora said, hoping she sounded nonchalant.

"Really?" Pamela was examining the papa doll. "I adore this fellow's smoking jacket."

"Rob wants to repay us for dinner by taking us out to eat at La Primo Bistro."

"That's nice. I hear they have good food. What day were the two of you thinking of going on this date?"

"It isn't a date," Nora insisted.

"Sounds like it to me."

"You were invited, too. I know it's very short notice but he asked if we could make it tomorrow night. I told him I would have to check with you."

"Tomorrow?" Pamela caught her lower lip between her teeth.

Nora swallowed her disappointment. "You have other plans."

"I do, but you can still go."

"I'm certainly not going if you can't make it. Inviting him to dinner was your idea in the first place."

"Okay, I think dinner at La Primo Bistro sounds like a wonderful idea. Call him and tell him it's fine with me."

"Are you sure?" Nora didn't want Pamela to feel like she was being pressured into going.

"I'm sure. I'll just call my friend. We can see a movie some other time. After all, Rob isn't going to be here that long."

"No, he isn't." Some of Nora's excitement dimmed. Rob would be leaving next week. She should be glad. Only, she found herself wishing he would stay.

And if he could? What then?

Chapter Ten

Rob had to admit that he hadn't felt this nervous before a date since high school. Probably not even then. As he held open the restaurant door for Nora and Pamela, he hoped it didn't show.

Inside, he glanced around at the elegant decor. Frescos on the walls depicted scenes from the different provinces of Italy. Small tables with white linen tablecloths were grouped around a large fountain in the center of the room. Candles in red glass globes in the center of each table added to the ambiance.

As a waiter with an authentic Italian accent led them across the room to a table in a small alcove, Rob decided that if the food was as good as the setting, he was in for a treat.

As he pulled out Nora's chair, he couldn't

help but admire the way she looked in her stunning black dress. The waiter seated Pamela. She murmured her thanks but kept looking toward the entrance.

"What's good here?" Rob asked, checking out the menu with difficulty instead of feasting his eyes on Nora.

"I can recommend the calamari and the scallops." Nora lifted her fan-folded napkin from her plate and spread it on her lap.

When the waiter returned to take their order, Pamela said, "Nora, Rob, I know this is going to sound rude, but I'm not staying for dinner. My date just arrived."

"What?" Nora demanded, clearly stunned.

As the waiter retreated, Rob glanced in the direction Pamela was looking. A young man in his midtwenties stood just inside the entrance. He was dressed in a dark gray jacket over blue jeans. A string tie at his throat and the cowboy hat in his hands completed the outfit.

Pamela stood and dropped a kiss on Nora's cheek. "I knew you wouldn't come without me, but I really didn't want to change my plans with Gary. The two of you have a great evening. Rob, perhaps we can grab lunch sometime before you leave Prairie Springs."

He rose to his feet. "I'll make a point of it."

Pamela left and made her way between the tables toward the door. Her date broke into a wide beaming smile when he caught sight of her. Both of them waved as they headed out the door.

Rob glanced at Nora. Her cheeks were rosy red with embarrassment. She said, "I am mortified by my stepdaughter's behavior. I can't believe she would do this. I'm going to have a serious talk with her when she gets home."

"I'm sorry she upset you, but don't let it ruin your evening." He opened the menu. "You said the calamari is good. Let's start with that for an appetizer, shall we?"

"You're being very gracious about this."

He didn't feel gracious at all. He was positively delighted to finally find himself alone with Nora.

"Here's how I look at it. Pamela just cut my bill by a third. We can splurge and get the lobster."

A ghost of a smile curved her lips. "I thought you liked steak."

"No, I told Olga to choose a restaurant that served a good steak for her first date," he corrected. "I enjoy a good steak as much as the next guy, but I prefer seafood."

Nora, who was looking toward the door, drew in a sharp breath. "It seems Olga didn't take your advice."

"What makes you say that?"

"Because she just came in with Pastor Fields."

Rob twisted around in his chair. Sure enough, the Reverend Frank Fields, dressed in somber shades of black, was standing beside Olga Terenkov as they waited to be seated. Olga was wearing a bold pink-and-white flowered dress. She had a bright pink shawl edged with foot-long fringe draped over her arms. A large star-burst necklace glittered at her throat. She looked like an exotic bird standing beside her date as she chatted away.

Rob turned back and leaned toward Nora, his eyes brimming with amusement. "Don't you think he looks nervous?"

Nora knew exactly what the minister was going through, but he couldn't possibly be more nervous than she was at this minute. While she wanted to be angry with Pamela for running off and leaving her alone with Rob, she had to admit she wasn't. Pamela had been right. Nora wouldn't have had the courage to come alone.

Rob would be leaving soon, and this might be her last opportunity to spend time alone with him. Determined to enjoy the evening, she was nonetheless glad to focus on Olga's situation instead of her own. She said, "Olga has a good heart, but she can be a bit flamboyant."

Rob leaned closer to Nora. "How does it look like it's going for them?"

Sending a covert glance over his shoulder toward Olga and Pastor Frank, Nora knew what Olga was feeling, too—excitement and nervous energy.

"They're just being shown to their table. Should we make ourselves known?"

"Not unless they notice us. Let them enjoy each other's company without thinking they're being watched. What's happening now?"

"Robert Dale, stop being a nosy reporter," she chided.

"I can't help it. Act nonchalant and tell me what they're doing. Better yet, trade places with me."

"No, then I couldn't see. They're being shown to a table by the fountain." Quickly, she raised her menu in front of her face. "Olga is looking this way."

Nora giggled, feeling daring and silly at the same time, but for once she didn't care. She wanted to enjoy an evening in Rob's company and forget that they didn't have anything in common or any kind of future.

"Don't keep me in suspense. What's going

on?" he demanded in a low voice vibrating with suppressed laughter.

Nora raised up to peek over her menu. Her eyes widened with surprise. "Olga is hugging another man."

Rob raised both eyebrows. "Whoa. That can't be good."

Rob wasn't as interested in how Olga's big date was going as he was in watching Nora. He'd never seen her so carefree and relaxed. She looked genuinely happy as she delved into their game of make-believe espionage. Someday, he would have to tell Olga how indebted he was to her for this evening.

"I'm sure the man is an old friend or someone from her church—although he looks like a pro wrestler," Nora whispered.

"Maybe he's an old boyfriend trying to steal her away from the good minister."

Nora lowered her menu and leaned forward, a perplexed frown on her face. "What on earth is going on?"

Rob turned to look. Olga and a beefy-looking man with bleached blond hair combed straight back were still toe to toe, but they had their hands at their throats. He couldn't imagine what they were doing. "I have no idea."

Soon, the pastor and a nearby woman customer joined the pair, all with their hands working on something between Olga and the unknown man. It wasn't until the woman stepped behind Olga that Rob realized she was trying to unlatch Olga's necklace. A second later, Olga stepped away, leaving her starburst necklace dangling from a thick gold chain that encircled her friend's neck.

Rob and Nora looked at each other and both tried to stifle their mirth behind their hands.

"We shouldn't be laughing." Nora gave him a stern look, but neither of them could keep a straight face.

Working hard to keep his chuckles contained, he opened his menu and pretended to study it. "For the main course I'm going to have the lobster. What about you?"

"I'm thinking of having the sea bass." Her voice quivered, but she managed to suppress her amusement. "Poor Olga. How embarrassing."

"Did she get her necklace back yet?"

"I'm afraid to look." She leaned slightly to the side to look around him. "They made it to their table. Let's hope things go smoothly for them for the rest of the evening."

"Amen." Rob looked over his shoulder. Olga,

intent on speaking to her date, had leaned toward him at the small, intimate table. She was toying with the ends of her shawl and didn't seem to notice how close the fringe was to the candle until the dangling trim made contact and burst into flames.

Olga shrieked and dropped the fabric on the tables. She shot to her feet and spun away as Pastor Fields beat at the burning material with his napkin. Olga stumbled backward into the low rim of the fountain. She teetered and flailed wildly for an instant. A passing waiter tried to grab her and missed, losing control of the tray he balanced overhead in the process. As Olga fell into an undignified heap in the shallow water, the tray with several loaded plates crashed to the floor, sending the sound of shattering china reverberating through the restaurant. Rob and Nora both leaped up to help.

Rob's heart went out to Olga as he and Pastor Fields assisted the dripping woman out of the fountain, ignoring the crowd gathering around them. Pulling off his jacket, Pastor Frank draped it over her shoulders.

"Are you all right?" Nora asked, clearly concerned about her. "Did you hit your head?"

Olga straightened and pushed her hair out of her eyes. "Nothing's hurt except my pride."

Glancing down at her sodden clothes, she gave Pastor Frank a wry smile. "It's a good thing this dress is wash and wear."

Her friend, the jewelry-wearing bodybuilder, muscled his way through the crowd. "Olga, darling, are you injured?" he demanded in a thick Russian accent.

"I'm fine. Really. Everyone, I'm okay. I'd just like to go home."

"Of course." Frank took her elbow and began steering her gently through the crowd.

By now the restaurant management had arrived and order was restored quickly as the broken plates were swept up and a fresh table-cloth replaced the charred one.

Nora and Rob returned to their table, but their easy laughter had dissipated. He could only hope that Olga's mishap hadn't ruined his evening as well.

Olga's first-date disaster put a damper on Nora's mood and forced her to take a closer look at what loomed in store for her. Pastor Frank and Olga's romantic future didn't look bright, but at least there was still a faint glimmer of hope for them. They lived and worked in the same town. They shared common values. She and Rob had nothing in common.

There was no future for them beyond the next few days.

Trying to pretend that tonight would be enough had been foolish. All she was doing was courting heartache. Resolving to remain detached and guard the wall she had built around her heart, she bit down on her lip to stop its quivering.

Suddenly, Rob reached across the table and covered her hand with his own. "What's wrong?"

His touch made her heart contract with longing. Why did he make her wish for things she knew would never be hers? Tears threatened, but she blinked them away. "I'm just feeling sorry for Olga. She was anticipating tonight with such happiness and look how it turned out."

"I'll grant you that isn't the way I'd like to end our evening, but every relationship is filled with ups and downs. If the pastor is a brave, wise man, and I think he is, he'll see that Olga is a woman of great faith and fortitude. She certainly showed grace under pressure here tonight. If she wanted to make a lasting impression on him, I think she managed that."

"I hope you're right."

"I am. Now, let's order, and to make sure our evening doesn't end in disaster, I'm going to blow out this candle." He leaned forward and extinguished it with a single puff.

Nora smiled, but she knew it wouldn't be a candle that spelled disaster for her. Her growing feelings for Rob could only lead to pain. Sharing those feelings wouldn't be possible. A strong relationship had to be built on trust and honesty, two qualities she was sadly lacking.

After the waiter took their order, Rob sat back in his chair. "Tell me about yourself, Nora."

Oh, how she wished she could. She picked up her water glass and took a sip before she answered. "What is there to tell that you don't already know?"

"A million things. Are you a Cowboys fan? Do you like buffalo wings? Do you like Texas?"

They were all safe topics, and she relaxed a fraction. "Texas is…big. It takes a little getting used to, but yes, I like it. I'm not a sports fan and I don't care for buffalo wings. What about you?"

"I like all kinds of sports, I'd rather have buffalo wings than a burger and I think Texas is growing on me. I certainly like Prairie Springs."

Did she really want to know why? Wouldn't it be better to skip even this casual exchange of personal information? Still, she couldn't help asking, "Why is that?"

"I like the small-town atmosphere. I like the patriotism and the feeling that our men and women in the service are accorded the respect that they deserve here. I like that people show pride in their country here. I also like that a lot of people here do more than pay lip service to their faith. They put it into action."

"Your faith means a lot to you, doesn't it?" Setting her glass down, she used her napkin to dab at the corner of her mouth. What would it be like to believe so strongly in something other than herself?

"Yes, it does. It could mean a lot to you, too, if you gave God a chance."

"I gave God a chance once."

"What happened?"

Suddenly his question wasn't casual but deeply private. Going back to that time in her life was so painful, yet she suspected that he would understand.

"I prayed once for Him to save someone I loved. Praying didn't make a bit of difference. Besides, if He is such a loving father, why do I see so many children with defective hearts?"

"I'm sorry for your loss, Nora. It's true that there is suffering in this world. I won't deny that, but once we accept God's love and His forgiveness, we can bear anything. He doesn't promise us that we won't have pain. He only promises that He will be there to comfort us no matter what."

"But as a soldier, how did you face death and suffering and not question that belief?"

"You give me too much credit. I've had my share of doubts. I'm only human."

"How did you get past those doubts?" She wanted to understand him. To do that meant understanding how he saw his faith. Her resolve to remain detached began slipping away.

"I guess I kept my heart open to Him."

"What do you mean by that?"

"We can't see God's love any more than we can see the radiation that produces the X-rays you use, but the love is there the same way your radiation is there."

"We have film that provides the proof that X-rays exist. There is no proof that God exists." Her sarcasm sounded hollow, even to her own ears.

"There's no proof that He doesn't. Sometimes I see proof of His love more when I'm not looking for it. Take Ali as an example."

Scowling at him, she asked, "How can you

use that child's tragic life as an example of God's plan? The boy lost everything."

"At first glance it does seem that way, but widen the picture. General Willis and his son never reconciled before his son was killed. If Ali hadn't been orphaned and injured, Marlon Willis would never have known his only grandson. Now, Ali's bright eyes and shy smile have helped an old man find comfort and closure to his son's death. We have no idea what other gifts Ali has to bestow on those his life will touch now."

Nora fingered the locket she always wore. She had been grief stricken after losing Bernard and her baby girl. Her focus then had been her own heartbreak and on Pamela's suffering. Later, she had allowed bitterness to creep in and replace the love she had known. Exploring the possibility that God was using all of them for something greater was a hard concept to take in.

"It would be comforting to think that some good will come out of Ali's sad experience, but I'm not sure I see how it can."

"Because you only see with human eyes. The good that comes out of this may not even be in our lifetime, Nora, but it is there. Faith makes it possible to believe that. God can heal anything."

"I hear that all the time. Usually before

someone is depending on me to fix their child's bad heart. God should do His own repairs."

"He is, Nora. You are the tool He uses whether you admit it or not."

She wanted to accept that what Rob said was true, but she was afraid. She was afraid to give up her grief. She was afraid to admit that she wasn't in control of her life.

"Is it so hard to accept that you are an instrument of God's love?" Rob asked gently. "That you have been placed here, exactly where you are needed the most, with exactly the right skills?"

She shook her head. "If that were true I would be able to save every child. I believe in science and in the things I can see and touch."

"Pamela said that you do needlework."

Taken aback by his abrupt change of topic, she sent him a puzzled look. "What does that have to do with religion?"

"Then you know what a tapestry is."

"Of course. It's a woven picture or pattern made to hang on a wall."

"Exactly. I once saw one of a lion. It was full of beautiful colors of gold, blacks and browns and only two small dots of white. Those white dots were in the eyes of the lion and it made him seem to be staring straight at me."

"I'm not following you."

"Think of our lives as threads in a tapestry of infinite size. Your life, my life, everyone's life is a colored thread being woven into a great cloth. As the thread we can't see the pattern. Only the weaver, God, knows what the picture will look like."

She'd never thought of her life as part of a greater whole. "You're saying our individuality doesn't matter."

"No. I'm saying that without those two dots of white thread the lion would have been pretty, but it wouldn't have seemed alive. They changed everything."

Nora touched the locket she wore. "Even a brief life has a purpose," she said quietly.

"I believe that with all my heart. Nora, why don't you come to church with me on Sunday?"

She shook her head. "I don't know. It's been such a long time. It wouldn't feel right."

"Give God a chance. If you don't feel comfortable, you can leave. Take my word for it, they don't lock the doors to keep the flock in."

"I'll think about it."

"Good." He sat back with a satisfied grin. "I'll pick you up at nine."

"If I decide I want to leave or I get paged to the hospital, then you would have to leave, too."

"I won't mind, honest. Fair enough?"

"You're persuasive, I'll give you that."

"Each of us seeks God in our own way, so it really isn't me. It's your heart looking to find answers. Maybe the Lord just put me here as a sort of signpost to point you in the right direction."

Was he right? There had been times in surgery when she felt as if some greater force were guiding her hands. She had known patients that survived and thrived against all odds.

Nora wanted to believe that she had a purpose beyond the successes and failures of her own life, but how could she ever really be sure?

A small voice at the back of her mind whispered, *By faith.*

Whistling happily, Rob let himself into his motel room later that night after taking Nora home from the restaurant. The evening spent with her would have to qualify as one of his most memorable, and not just because of Olga's mishap.

Tossing his keys on the dresser, he kicked off his shoes and dropped onto the bed. Crossing his arms behind his head, he lay and stared at ceiling.

He couldn't stop thinking about the way Nora looked tonight—how pretty she was when she smiled, the way a small furrow creased her forehead when she was concentrating. She had an adorable giggle.

It seemed like he discovered something new and special about her each time they were together. He'd known a lot of women in his time, but he'd never met anyone who made him feel the way she did. He might never grow tired of watching her eyes light up when she was happy.

Even though she hadn't given him a yes or no answer about attending church with him, he was still hopeful. Faith was the path to true happiness. Rob wanted to help her discover that for herself.

He glanced at the red numbers of the clock radio beside the bed. It was late, but sleep was the last thing on his mind. Sitting up, he pulled his laptop from the bedside stand and opened the lid. The message that he had new mail prompted him to open the program. One of the messages was from Carter. Rob tapped the mouse to open the e-mail

Scanning the brief note quickly, Rob saw that the young reporter had done a good job talking to everyone he could find who was involved with Children of the Day on his end. His list of contacts was impressive. He might be new to the area, but he was methodical. Carter had gotten statements from aid workers, clergy and medical personnel all praising the work done by the small Texas charity. It wasn't until Rob reached the end of the missive that he frowned and reread the sentence.

The doctor here is particularly grateful for the case of antibiotics that arrived yesterday. He says one thousand vials of penicillin will help stem the spread of a serious infection among the infants and children. He sends his thanks and prayers for more medicines.

One thousand? Rob distinctly remembered Nora negotiating for four thousand vials of antibiotics. What had happened to the rest of it?

He tried to think if Anna or anyone else had mentioned how many drugs had been sent. All he could recall was Nora saying she would handle the shipping herself. Had Tarkott Pharmaceutical sent less than promised? Wouldn't Nora have mentioned it if that were the case?

Rob typed a quick question. Are you sure he only received one thousand vials?

He hit Send and bit his thumbnail as he waited for an answer. He glanced at the clock as the minutes slowly ticked by for almost an hour. At last, the incoming mail chime sounded, and he clicked open Carter's answer.

The doctor definitely said one thousand. Why?

An uneasy sensation settled in Rob's stomach that had nothing to do with the lobster he'd had for dinner. He typed another note to Carter.

Four thousand vials were shipped. See if you can discover where the holdup is on your end. Call me when you get an answer. I don't care what time it is here. Rob typed in his cell phone number and hit Send.

The most likely explanation was that the cases of drugs had simply become separated during the overseas shipping process. They would probably show up in a day or two. If they didn't, Rob would take a much closer look to find out why.

Chapter Eleven

Rob's cell phone started ringing just as he was opening the motel room door on Saturday afternoon. He tossed his pillowcase full of clean laundry on the bed and pulled the phone from his pocket, knowing it was his boss by the ring tone he had set. He wanted it to be Carter calling to tell him the rest of the drugs from Children of the Day had arrived. It was irrational to expect an answer in less than twelve hours. Rob knew he had to be patient awhile longer.

"Dale here," he mumbled, balancing the phone between his ear and his shoulder as he dumped his clothes onto the bed and began sorting them to put them away.

"Are you still at Fort Bonnell?"

"Hello to you, too, Derrick."

"Yes or no?"

Rob raked a hand through his hair and sat down on the edge of the bed. His boss obviously wasn't in the mood for humor. "Yes, I'm still here."

"Great. There's a story coming in over the wire about the newlywed soldiers that have been missing for the last few months."

"The Harpswell couple?"

"Right. The husband has been found."

"Alive?" Rob held his breath.

"Yes, alive. Amazing, isn't it? I thought for sure they were both dead."

"What about his wife?"

"No sign of her. The guy was in pretty bad shape, but the word is that he's going to make it."

"Thank God. There are a lot of people praying for him here."

"Here, too. I want you to get local reaction to the news. Interview people the couple served with, you know the drill. The wife has family in the area, doesn't she?"

"Yes, a brother."

"Great. Get an interview with him."

"I'll try."

"Don't try. Do it."

"Where is John? I'd like to give the brother and the people at Children of the Day as much information as I can."

"He's being medevaced to Germany. From what I gather, the guy doesn't remember anything that happened. They're hoping it is temporary amnesia, but who knows."

"That's rough. His wife is still missing and he's the one person who might know what happened to her."

"It isn't the news everyone is praying for, but it's good news nonetheless."

"Where did they find him?"

"Some local herdsmen found him wandering in the foothills about fifty miles north of where the convoy was ambushed."

Rob already had a mental picture of the area. It was rugged, nearly inaccessible terrain. He had crisscrossed the area on horseback and on foot two years before while following leads on a terrorist training camp.

"I'll get a story to you ASAP," Rob promised.

"That's what I'm paying you for." The line went dead and Rob closed the phone.

Leaving his laundry on the bed, Rob grabbed his keys and headed out the door. Anna and Olga deserved to know about John Harpswell as soon as possible. Ten minutes later, Rob pulled up in front of the Children of the Day offices and hurried up the steps to ring the bell.

Olga answered the door dressed in jeans and

an oversized chambray shirt with the sleeved rolled up past her elbows. By the look on her face, Rob knew she had already heard the news. From the lobby he could hear the sound of the television playing. Over her shoulder she called out, "It's Rob Dale."

Anna appeared quickly from the other room. To Rob's surprise, Nora was with her. Olga grasped Rob's arm. "Have you heard that John Harpswell has been found?"

"I got a call from my boss a few minutes ago. What are they saying on the news channels?"

Anna answered him. "Only that John is injured and being flown to Germany for medical care. They aren't saying anything about Whitney. Do you know more?"

He followed the women inside where several staff member were clustered in front of the small television in the corner of the lobby. "I don't know much more than you do. The call I got said John Harpswell had been found wandering alone, that he had a serious head injury but he is expected to recover."

"And?" Nora prompted, studying him closely.

"He doesn't remember what happened."

Olga pressed a hand to her heart. "How awful, but thank God he is safe now. I'm sure the army is searching the area for signs of Whitney, too."

"It's a very rugged and remote area." Rob tried not to sound discouraging, but he didn't want to hold out false hope.

"I should call Evan Paterson," Olga said suddenly. "He's Whitney's brother. He has been in limbo not knowing what happened to her, and now he has to face more uncertainty. I'm going to see if there is anything we can do." Olga quickly left the room.

"Amnesia is not uncommon after head trauma," Nora said quietly. "Did they say what kind of injury it was?"

"No. What are you doing here?"

"I stopped by to make sure Olga was okay after her disaster of a date last night."

"Is she?" he asked, glancing toward where Olga stood with the secretary's phone pressed to her ear. The other staff members, including Anna, were still watching the latest on the television.

Nora nodded. "I would have been in tears, but she's as chipper as ever. She says it will make a great story for them to laugh about in years to come. The big man she was hugging is actually a distant cousin, by the way."

"It was nice of you to come."

Nora had surprised him yet again. The cool, detached doctor he'd met less than two weeks ago wasn't the caring friend he saw today. Was it Nora who had changed or was it his perception of her? Every time he learned something new about her it made him want to know more.

The realization that he was falling hard for her stuck him with sudden clarity.

Nora glanced at the others and then at Rob. "Are you going to stay here for a while?"

He forced his mind back to his job. "My paper wants me to interview people who know or have served with John and Whitney and get their reactions to this news. What about you?"

"I just got back from making rounds at the hospital. I was thinking about taking Conan for a run in the park. I was going to ask if you wanted to join us, but I see that you have to work."

"Would you like to tag along with me instead?"

"On interviews?"

"Yeah. I've been into surgery with you. Now is your chance to see me doing my job."

She hesitated and he was afraid she would say no, but after a moment, she smiled and said, "Okay. Where are you going to start?"

Just then, Olga came back into the room. "Evan is on his way here. He wants to talk to you, Rob. I told him you were familiar with the area where John was found."

"I'll be happy to talk to him, but I don't know that I can add anything to what he already knows."

Olga sighed heavily. "Evan needs to feel that he is doing something—anything—to help find his sister. He has a ranch just outside of town. He'll be here as soon as he can get someone to stay with his daughter. In the meantime, can I get you some iced tea or something to drink?"

Rob glanced at Nora. She shook her head, so he said, "No, we're good."

"All right then, I'll be with the others if you need me."

Twenty minutes later, there was a loud knock at the door. Leaving his seat in front of the television, Rob walked to the entryway. He quickly assessed the man Anna showed into the room.

Evan Paterson was tall with sandy-brown hair and the rugged features of a man who spent his days outdoors. He came toward Rob with purposeful strides and held out his hand. "Thanks for seeing me, Mr. Dale."

"Not a problem."

"I understand that you're a reporter for the *Liberty and Justice*."

"That's true, but I hope you won't hold it against me. I'd like to do an interview with you about your sister, but I know this may not be the best time."

"You're the first reporter I've met that cared whether it was a good time or not. Most of them just pepper me with the same questions over and over again. Olga tells me that you know the area where John was found."

"Please, have a seat," Rob suggested, leading the way back into the lobby. "Yes, I've spent time in the area. It isn't an easy place to search."

Evan sank onto the edge of a chair and leaned forward, his blue eyes searching Rob's face. "I'll give you an exclusive interview if you'll tell me what you know about the area."

"The closest thing to the terrain that we have in this country is the badlands. It's rugged and harsh. It's an easy place to get lost."

"But you found your way around it."

"I was trained to survive in that kind of environment, and I had local tribesmen to guide me."

"Will they help the army?"

"Maybe. The problem is that the people there distrust strangers."

"You must know someone who will help. Please, I'm begging you."

The odds of finding anything about the missing woman after all this time were slim to none unless John Harpswell recovered his memory. Rob did know men who crisscrossed that hostile region, but they were gunrunners and smugglers. They wouldn't talk to just anyone.

If he gave Carter access to his Middle East contacts and the young reporter uncovered something about Whitney Harpswell, Rob knew he could kiss his hopes of reassignment goodbye. Carter would be able to keep the Middle East post for as long as he wanted.

Rob drew a deep breath and let it out slowly. "I might know someone. Let me make a few calls."

Nora waited for Rob as he shook hands with Evan on the steps of the building. As Evan walked to his truck parked on the street, Nora moved to stand beside Rob. "Do you really think your friend can find her?"

"Honestly, I doubt it, but it's worth a try."

"What are you going to do?"

"Our paper has a reporter in the capital. If I give Carter the names of some of my old contacts and vouch for him, he may be able to uncover some new information."

"Is he the man who got the job you wanted?"

"That's the one. I may be helping him keep the job I want, but what choice do I have? Even the remote possibility that I could help discover the fate of that woman is worth more than any job. You saw the look in Evan's eyes. He'd do anything for his sister."

"What if your reporter friend doesn't turn up anything?"

"Then Whitney Harpswell's fate remains in God's hands and we've done everything humanly possible."

Nora reached out and took his hand. She had been wrong to be afraid of him. Lacing her fingers through his, she gave a gentle squeeze. "You're a good man, Robert Dale."

His eyes met hers and darkened with deep emotion. "I'm glad you think so."

"I'm going to miss you when you leave."

A grin tugged up the corner of his mouth. "Is this the same woman that wouldn't give me the time of day two weeks ago?"

"No," Nora answered sincerely. "I'm not the same woman at all, and I have you to thank for that."

To her delight, he leaned down and kissed her.

The world dropped away, leaving the two of them alone as a feeling of rightness engulfed her and sent her heart spinning. Gently, he cupped her face in his hands and drew away. Gazing into her eyes, he whispered, "I like the new Nora."

"The new Nora likes you, too."

His grin widened. "I'm in unfamiliar territory here. What happens next?"

The buzzing of her pager brought her back to earth with a thump. She pulled the device from the pocket of her jacket and scrolled through the message all the while wishing that Rob would kiss her again. Her bubble of happiness subsided when she saw she was needed back at Mercy Medical Center.

"I'm sorry, Rob, I have to get back to the hospital." Oh, how she wanted to stay with this man and share the happiness skipping through her veins.

"I hope it's nothing serious."

She forced herself to smile. "Serious is what I do best."

He stroked her cheek with his fingers. "I believe it is. Will I see you at church tomorrow?"

She hesitated. So much had happened so quickly. Was she willing to let God back into her life? Rob, Anna and Olga, they all made living their faith look so easy, but it wasn't. Giving her life over to God was a step Nora wasn't sure she knew how to take.

Rob seemed to sense her indecision. He reached out and drew her into his arms. She rested her cheek against his chest and listened to the strong beat of his heart beneath her ear. The tension in her body melted away.

"Nora, God is there for you whenever you need Him. I'm not trying to push you into doing something you aren't ready for."

"Thank you." She closed her eyes and inhaled the spicy, warm scent so uniquely Rob's own.

She felt him kiss the top of her head, then he said, "I have phone calls to make and interviews to do and you have to get to the hospital."

"I know," she admitted, but she didn't move.

For the first time in years, she permitted herself to give and to receive comfort from someone other than Pamela. Allowing her small universe to expand and include Rob meant trusting him. The prospect was as scary as it was exciting.

After several seconds, he slipped a finger under her chin and lifted her face to his. "Sweetheart, are you all right?"

Hearing him call her sweetheart sent a thrill of pleasure zinging to her core. The concern she saw in his eyes touched her deeply. Could she really be falling in love with this man? She barely knew him. It was all happening so quickly. Uncertainty reared its head. How could this be real?

Unbidden, the memory of Bernard's first kiss crept into her mind. She had trusted him and believed that she loved him. She had been convinced that he was a good man, too. It wasn't until later she found out how wrong she had been.

Taking a step back, she tried to gather her scattered wits. It was foolish to dream of becoming involved with Rob. As wonderful as it felt to rest in his arms, it could never be anything permanent. The fear of risking her heart again overshadowed the peace she found in Rob's embrace. She wasn't strong enough to take a chance on love again.

Brushing her hair back, she said, "Forgive me. I don't know what came over me."

She turned away, but he caught her arm in a gentle but firm grasp. "Nora, there are so many things I want to say to you, but this isn't the right time or the right place."

She managed a smile. "I don't think there is a right time or a right place for us."

"What does that mean?" The look of confusion on his face mirrored her own emotions.

"Why don't we just agree that we like each other and not look for anything more. I'm sorry if I gave you a different impression. I'll see you Monday when Ali checks into the hospital for his surgery."

As she hurried down the steps toward her car, she didn't know was if she was running away from or running toward a broken heart.

Chapter Twelve

Shortly after nine o'clock on Monday morning, Rob accompanied Ali, General Willis and Sarah Alpert to the pediatric floor at Mercy Medical Center. All of the adults bore worried expressions. Only Ali, walking beside his grandfather and holding the old man's hand, seemed unaware of the seriousness of the situation. Although his surgery wasn't until tomorrow, he would undergo more tests today to make sure he was strong enough to have it done. Under one arm, he clutched a brown teddy bear wearing a cowboy hat and boots.

When they had been shown to a room and Ali had changed into his pajamas, Marlon Willis sank into the recliner at the bedside with a deep sigh. His face was flushed and he seemed to be breathing hard. Sarah paused in the process of showing Ali how to make the head of the bed go up and down. She reached over and touched the general's shoulder. "Are you okay?"

Marlon's eyes flew open and he patted her hand. "I'm a little tired, that's all."

Rob settled himself into one of the chairs in the room and kept glancing toward the door. He knew Nora would be here to see Ali soon.

After a few minutes, two nurses entered. One said, "General Willis, we have some papers for you to sign at the nursing station. While you are doing that, we'll get Ali admitted."

Marlon heaved himself out of the recliner. He tousled Ali's hair. "I'll be back in a few minutes. You do what these ladies tell you to do."

Ali's eyes grew suddenly serious. "Yes, Grandpa."

The nurse looked at Rob and Sarah. "You'll have to step out as well."

Rob followed the general and Sarah to the main desk where another young nurse explained in detail the plans for the next day. When she was finished, the general asked a few questions, then signed the documents she slid across the desk to him.

Rob glanced down the hall and saw Nora walking toward him. She looked as beautiful as ever. He smiled when she met his gaze, and he walked toward her. Stopping in front of her, he said, "I was hoping to see you."

There was a wariness in her eyes that troubled him. Her smile was tight as she asked, "How have you been?"

"Not bad. And you?"

"I've been…okay. Is Ali and everyone ready for his big day?"

"He's the only one who isn't scared. Is there somewhere you and I can go to talk?" Rob wanted to speak to Nora alone. He wanted to tell he how much he had missed her the past two days.

"I'm really very busy. Perhaps another time."

The door of Ali's room opened and the nurses came out. Nora avoided looking at Rob and said, "I'd like to see Ali alone for a few minutes. Please tell his grandfather that I'll be out to talk to him shortly."

Rob nodded. "Sure."

He took a step back and shoved his hands in his hip pockets. She seemed so distant. He wanted to reach out and take hold of her hand, but she entered Ali's room before Rob could think of anything else to say.

Walking back to the desk, Rob told Sarah and Marlon what Nora had said. Together, they waited in the hall until Nora came out of the room. She avoided meeting Rob's eyes as she approached the general. "Do you have any questions about what we'll be doing tomorrow?"

He shook his head. "I just want to know that my grandson is going to be okay."

She clasped the chart tightly to her chest. Looking down, she said, "The statistics are certainly in his favor, but I can't make that promise. I'll see you before the surgery tomorrow."

She walked away quickly to confer with one of the nurses and together they entered another room. Rob watched her go with a sinking heart. Could she dismiss him so easily from her life? He didn't want to believe that any more than he wanted to believe that she was involved in stealing drugs.

"Maybe we should have found a doctor with more of a bedside manner," General Willis said, an unhappy scowl on his face.

"Nora is the best at what she does," Rob assured him.

"She had better be."

They reentered Ali's room to find him sitting up in bed with a big smile on his face. "Doctor Nora say she fix my heart tomorrow. She tell me good story."

"What story?" Rob asked, intrigued by Ali's lack of nervousness.

"She tell me how she fix my heart with little, how you say, oh, stitches. She show me Mr. Bear with broken heart and how she fix him. She fix me just the same."

Rob picked up the bear Ali kept beside him. "You mean this bear?"

"No. She keep her Mr. Bear to show other kids."

Rob and the general exchanged puzzled glances. Nora hadn't been carrying a toy.

Taking his teddy from Rob, Ali sat the toy on his lap. "She is nice lady, but I think she is sad, too."

"Why do you think that?" Rob asked gently.

"She asked me if I'm scared. When I tell her no because God and my mother will take care of me, too, she get tears in her eyes."

Nora finished her rounds in the PICU by eleven o'clock and walked toward her office. Her few patients were all doing well. If only she could say the same about herself.

Outside she might have appeared as calm as ever, but inside she waged a constant battle with her aching heart. Seeing Rob today only made her more aware of the depths of her feelings for him.

Yesterday, she had tried to shake thoughts of him by taking Conan for a run through the quiet streets of the town. It wasn't until she found herself outside the Prairie Springs Christian Church that Nora knew she hadn't succeeded.

As she stood looking at the steeple silhouetted against the bright blue Texas sky, she knew Rob would be inside, but she also knew that wasn't the only reason she was there. She wanted to go in.

She wanted to know the kind of peace and love that Rob talked about when he spoke about his faith. Rejecting God out of grief and anger had been easy when the pain of her loss was fresh. Now, she was afraid that God wouldn't want her in His house after all these years.

Having the dog at her side had kept her from stepping into the church. When she turned away, a heavy sense of loss had settled in her chest and it hadn't gone away—until she had been alone with Ali this morning.

The little boy's bravery and unshakable faith made her ashamed of her own behavior.

Pushing open her outer office door, Nora saw Delia coming out of Peter Kent's office. Sitting quietly in the chairs along the wall was a young couple with a baby sleeping in a carrier at their feet. They held each other's hand tightly.

Delia said, "The Pelletier family is here to see you."

"Thank you, Delia. Please show them into the exam room." Turning to the parents, Nora said, "I'll be with you in a few minutes."

She had already reviewed the findings of the baby's cardiologist. What she had to do now was give the waiting couple the surgical options open to their child. They had already been to two other surgeons, neither of whom would attempt the complex repair.

Inside her office, Nora leafed through the chart Delia had prepared. As usual, her secretary had included all the information she needed. Delia was nothing if not meticulous.

The outer door opened and Delia came in. "I need your signatures on a few things, Dr. Blake."

"Of course." Nora took the stack of papers and began signing beside the red flags Delia used to mark all the places that needed Nora's name. The amount of paperwork the office generated was staggering at times. Nora didn't envy Delia and Carmen the job of keeping it straight.

When she was finished with the papers, Nora handed them back to Delia. "Is that all?"

"For now."

The woman turned toward the door, but Nora called after her. "Delia, wait a minute."

Pausing with her hand on the doorknob, Delia looked at Nora over her shoulder. "What is it, Doctor?"

"I just wanted to tell you how much I appreciate the work you do for Dr. Kent and myself. We couldn't run this office without you."

Her usually implacable expression changed to one of surprise. "Why...thank you, Dr. Blake."

"You're welcome."

A mild puzzled expression remained on Delia's face as she left the office.

The next chart Nora picked up belonged to Ali Tabiz Willis. Glancing through the preoperative laboratory reports, Nora was satisfied that Ali was well enough to undergo open-heart surgery. There was no sign of the upper respiratory infection that had plagued him in the last few months. Keeping the buildup of fluid off his lungs with the use of potent drugs had been a delicate balancing act, but it was only a stopgap measure. He needed the tear in the membrane between the two large chambers of his heart repaired, and soon.

Unlike the baby in the next room, Ali's repair would be a simple one and the boy should be out of PICU in less than a week. He could be out of the hospital and home in less than a week and a half. Once Ali was home, Rob would leave, too.

Closing the file, Nora glanced around her office. Rob's presence was everywhere. She could see his cocky grin and the gleam of humor in his eyes as plainly as if he were standing in front of her. She could still hear the tenderness in his voice the first time he'd stood in this room and asked if she believed that God led her to become a surgeon in Austin. Was it only two weeks ago? That day she had denied God's role in shaping her life.

Now, she would tell the family in the other room that she could repair their child's defective heart. What if the course of her life had not been a set of random events but a series of circumstances meant to place her exactly here on exactly this day to save this baby?

The thought was mind-boggling and humbling.

Rising, Nora walked through the exam room door. Inside, she greeted the parents. "Hello, I'm Dr. Blake."

Moving directly to the small sink, she thoroughly washed her hands and dried them before turning around. The couple, both in their early thirties, looked tired and fearful. The baby began to fret and the mother reached down to lift him from his carrier. Smiling up at Nora with a mixture of hopefulness and maternal pride, Mrs. Pelletier lifted him to her lap and said, "This is our son, Jason."

The little boy, now four months old, was thin with a pale, mottled color to his skin that Nora saw all too often. He stopped fussing when his mother began bouncing him and opened his eyes. Large and dark with thick lashes rimming them, he focused on his mother's face and opened his mouth in a sweet smile.

Nora held out her arms. "May I?"

"Certainly." The mother handed her child over, and Nora gathered the baby into her arms.

He was so light. Nora had forgotten how small and yet how perfect an infant could feel in her arms. Usually, she had the mother place the child on the exam table. This was the first baby she had held since Sondra's death. The pain of her loss was still there, still a part of her past, but this child belonged to the present and to the future if she were skilled enough.

With enormous wide eyes, Jason studied Nora and then decided she wasn't the one he wanted. He puckered up into a frown, but Nora cooed and rocked him until he settled.

Blinking back the tears that stung her eyes, she managed a smile for the worried couple staring at her. "I've looked at Jason's X-rays and echocardiograms and I believe I can do a repair. Does next Tuesday work for you?"

Leaning on the railing outside his motel room that evening, Rob turned his jacket collar up against the chill in the air. He glanced at his watch. It was ten o'clock.

He should make an early night of it, but he knew he couldn't sleep. Thoughts of Ali and his surgery scheduled for the morning kept Rob's mind racing. That and thoughts of Nora.

What was she doing tonight? How was she preparing? Or had she done so many of these operations that they no longer bothered her and she simply took them in stride? Somehow, he didn't think that was true.

For Rob, the waiting had always been the hard part. He wanted to get on with the action, get into battle, confront the bad guys or get to the bottom of the story. Now, he was discovering exactly how difficult waiting really was.

A light drizzle began falling. The wind blew the cold moisture against his face. It was a brisk reminder that October was almost gone and winter was just around the corner.

And Nora was just across town.

Straightening, he shoved his hand in his jacket pockets. His time here was drawing to a close but he wasn't ready to leave. His feelings for Nora were something that he wanted to explore. He didn't want a next assignment if it took him away from her. He stared out into the half-empty parking lot.

Half-empty, the same way his heart felt. He'd finally met a woman who might fill that emptiness and he didn't know what to do about it. His feelings for Nora had quickly become more than friendship on his part, but he faced the fact that she had never really opened up to him. He always felt she was keeping something back. Why? How could he reach her?

He glanced over his shoulder into his room and decided it would be useless to call it a night. Instead, he walked down the steps at the end of the landing and over to his truck. Getting in, he started the engine without any real plan in mind. He didn't know where he was going, but he knew where he wanted to be.

A few minutes later, he turned his vehicle onto the street where Nora lived and pulled up in front of her house.

The lights were on, and the sight made him bold enough to approach. Shoulders hunched against the drizzle, he rang the bell and waited.

Pamela opened the door, a look of surprise on her face. "Rob, what are you doing here?"

"That's a good question. I'll let you know when I have an answer. Is Nora here?"

Pamela stepped back from the door, inviting him in. "She's downstairs in her studio. Go on down. I think she'll be glad to see you."

As he took the steps to the lower level, he paused on the last step in surprise at the sight spread out before him. He hadn't known what she did in her retreat, but the long tables with a dozen dollhouses down the center of the room was the last thing he expected to see.

Nora was seated with her back to him and her loupes on. He couldn't see what she was doing. Conan lay on the floor beside her with his head resting on her foot. He looked up at Rob and wagged his stump of a tail, then yawned and lay down again.

Rob suddenly wondered if he should be here at all. He started to turn away when one of the figures in the dollhouse nearest him caught his attention. It was a little boy with dark hair and dark eyes. He was seated on a rocking horse with a teddy bear riding in front of him.

Rob picked up the miniature bear and stared at it in awe. There were tiny patches on his fur as if his owner had been too hard on the toy. A brown cloth patch covered the sole of one foot and a red patch had been sewn on his chest. Rob looked closer. The red patch was in the shape of a broken heart with both pieces mended together with incredibly fine stitches.

He glanced at Nora and found she was looking at him with an odd smile on her face. She said, "I call him Mr. Bear."

"Ali mentioned meeting him." Rob walked toward her and gestured around the room. "This is quite a collection you have. Did you make them all?"

"I buy the people and the houses, then I decorate the homes and make the clothing for the dolls to portray different eras."

"I've never seen anything like this."

"It's a hobby."

"I thought your hobby was crewel embroidery."

"If you'll take a look at the sofa and footstool in this house you'll see examples of my crewel-work."

He moved to stand beside her, and she handed him the pieces she was talking about. The intricate, tiny stitches were amazingly complex.

He glanced at her. "Have you always done this?"

She turned away and placed the doll she was working on into the bright yellow kitchen of the house beside her. "Pamela and I brought the first house together when I was pregnant. She wanted to give it to her new baby sister, but her sister never made it home from the hospital."

Stunned at the pain in her trembling voice, Rob knelt beside her chair. "What happened?"

Nora touched the locket she wore. "Sondra was born with a heart defect. One that couldn't be fixed. She died when she was three days old."

"I'm so sorry."

She looked into his eyes. "Thank you. I've been wanting to tell you about her, but the time never seemed right."

"Tell me now. I'm listening."

"She's the reason I became a pediatric heart surgeon. She's my constant reminder of how easily a child can slip away. Each time I talk to parents about what might happen to their son or daughter in surgery, I'm really trying to prepare them for the heartbreaking, soul-killing pain they might have to face, but my words never come out right." She bowed her head. "Why is that, Rob?"

He gently swept her hair back her from her face so that she would look at him. "I don't know. Maybe because you weren't born with the gift of gab the way I was?"

She gave him a tentative, grateful smile and his heart went out to her. "I've looked at your surgical outcomes, Nora. You save ninety-eight out of every one hundred children that come to you."

"No, I lose two lives out of every one hundred that I'm trying to save. That's two families destroyed forever."

He glanced at all the houses and the figures inside. "So that's why you do this. You're making families that will last forever."

She held up the dress she had made to fit one of her dolls. "You're right. I come here to create perfect families frozen in time. The little boys will ride their tricycles or rocking horses forever. The little girls will play with their dolls or their puppies. Fathers will read their papers in their favorite chairs and mothers will be cooking in the kitchen. No one down here dies. No one ever has to grieve."

He took the dress from her hand and laid it aside, then he grasped her fingers. "None of them ever sees the beauty of a sunrise. They may not know sadness, but they don't know joy. None of them love and are loved in return. They don't have perfect lives. They don't have life at all."

She looked away. "I know."

Putting one finger beneath her chin, he lifted

her face until she met his gaze. "We can only make the best of what we are given, Nora. I've been given the chance to know you and that makes me blessed. I find myself wanting to share everything beautiful with you."

Biting her lip, Nora stared at Rob without speaking as tears welled up in her eyes. Having him here was so right. Having him learn about her secret retreat and about Sondra gave Nora a sense of peace that she hadn't known in many years.

He understood what she had gone through, and someday soon she would tell him the rest. For now, knowing he cared was enough.

"I feel the same way about you, Rob. I never thought it was possible, but you have changed my life."

"Tell me you'll give what we have a chance to grow."

"I'd like that."

The relief on his face made her smile. He gripped her hands more tightly. "Nora, I love your spunk and the way you've dedicated your life to caring for children. I even like your dog, although he's chewing on my shoe at the moment."

Her eyes widened and she looked down. "Conan, don't do that."

Conan looked up as if surprised that he wasn't allowed to have expensive running shoes for a snack. He still had one white shoe-string dangling from his mouth.

Nora met Rob's eyes and both of them began to chuckle. Taking her face between his hands, Rob said, "It's a small price to pay for a chance to kiss you."

She smiled sweetly. "Since you've paid the toll, I think you'd better collect your prize."

He leaned forward and covered her lips with his own. Nora gave herself up to the joy racing through her veins.

Chapter Thirteen

As Rob entered Ali's hospital room on Tuesday morning, the sight of all the people clustered around the boy's bed took him aback. Besides General Willis and Sarah Alpert, he recognized Anna and her fiancé, David Ryland. With them were Caitlin Villard, army chaplain Steve Windham and Pastor Fields, all of whom he had met while doing his interviews about Children of the Day, and of course Olga.

Ali was holding the hand of chestnut-haired woman who stood beside his bed. With his free hand, the boy motioned Rob over. "This is my pretty Nurse Maddie."

Walking up to Ali, Rob leaned down and whispered, "You're right. She's very pretty."

"Pretty, but taken." A middle-aged man with a cane came to stand beside Maddie and lay a hand on her shoulder. "Hello, I'm Jake Hopkins. I'm the general's attorney and a friend of Ali's."

"A pleasure to meet you," Rob said, returning Jake's strong handshake.

Rob glanced around. These people, from all walks of life, had banded together to see that one little boy from a village halfway around the world had a chance at a new life. God's work was truly being done here.

The door to the room opened and Nora walked in with a chart in her hand. She looked up and her eyes widened at the sight of such a crowd in the room. Looking apologetic, she said, "I'm sorry, but I'm going to have to ask all of you to step out. Everyone but immediate family should go to the surgical waiting area."

"Of course, Doctor," Pastor Fields said, "but before we go, we would like to offer a prayer for Ali's recovery."

"Certainly."

Rob reached for Nora. She smiled softly as she laid her hand in his. Olga came to take Nora's other hand, a gentle look of happiness shining in her eyes. Pastor Frank and Chaplain Steve laid their hands on Ali. Around the room, the others joined hands and bowed their head.

"Heavenly Father," Pastor Frank began. "We

are gathered here to ask for Your blessings on this child. Make him whole and well again if that is Your will. Give us the strength to face what is to come and lend us Your comfort. Through Your Son, Jesus, our salvation is secured and all things are possible. Be with this child today. Hold him in the palm of Your hand. Lend Your strength and wisdom to his doctors and nurses. Let them become the instruments of Your healing power. We ask this in Jesus' name. Amen."

A chorus of amens filled the room. Rob looked up and found Nora watching him intently. His heart expanded with love. If the room hadn't been full of people he would have told her that very instant that he wanted to be part of her life forever.

General Willis's cell phone rang and he stepped away from the bed to answer it, but then quickly turned back to his grandson. "Ali, I have someone special here who wants to talk to you. Does anyone here know how to turn up the volume on this thing so we can all hear him?"

"I do." Chaplain Steve took it from him and after a few seconds said, "That should be it."

"Thank you." The general took it from him and set it down on the overbed table in front of Ali. "Go ahead, son. You're on speaker now."

"Ali, can you hear me?" A man's deep voice came over the line amid a few crackles of static.

Behind him, Rob heard a quick indrawn breath. Looking over his shoulder, he saw Sarah press a hand to her chest. She caught his eye and managed to quickly compose her face, but not before he saw that she clearly recognized the caller.

"Dr. Mike, is that you?" Ali demanded in disbelief.

"It's me, little buddy." The army surgeon's voice reverberated with emotion. "Sorry I can't be with you today, but I'm thinking about you and wishing you the best. I know you'll do fine."

"I'm thinking for you, too, Dr. Mike."

Rob smiled at the boy's mangled English. This call would need to be included in his story. That Dr. Michael Montgomery was calling from a war zone half the world away to wish the boy well proved how much Ali had touched his life.

Rob looked around the room. This child had touched so many lives. He prayed Nora's gift would allow him to touch many more in ways only God knew.

After the call ended, everyone filed out to make their way down to the surgical waiting area. Rob stepped aside, hoping for a few minutes with Nora before she left to get ready. He didn't have long to wait.

She came out with one of the nurses. After giving some additional instructions on what she wanted done before Ali left for the pre-op area, Nora closed the chart she held and handed it over. When the woman walked away, Nora turned and smiled at Rob. The sight warmed his heart.

"Everything looks good," she said.

"You look good," he said, reaching to take hold of her hand and pulling her toward the open door of an empty room. Inside, he turned to face her. Gathering both her hands in his, he smiled and said, "In fact, you look great."

Grinning widely, she rolled her eyes in amusement. "Flattery will get you nowhere."

"I beg to differ. It got me a few minutes alone with you, didn't it?"

"I'm working, Rob." She tried to sound stern, but all he heard was a huskiness in her tone that sent his heart into overdrive.

Sighing heavily, he said, "I know. Just promise me that we can continue this later."

Rising on tiptoe, she planted a kiss on his cheek. "Later, I promise."

"I'll walk you down to surgery," he offered, not wanting her out of his sight.

"I have other patients to see. Ali won't actually go into the surgical suite for another hour or so. I'll meet you down there. Until then, get a cup of that caramel coffee you like so much."

He squeezed her hands. "All right, but you can't get rid of me for long."

"I was hoping you would say that."

His cell phone began ringing. Nora raised one eyebrow. "You'll have to release my hand to answer that."

"It can go to voice mail."

Tugging free, she gave him a rueful smile. "It might be important."

He shook his head. "More important than spending a stolen minute with you? I don't think so."

"You really do know how to flatter a woman. Answer your calls while you can. You'll have to turn your phone off before you go into surgery. It can interfere with some of our equipment."

She gave him a quick peck on the cheek and walked out of the room. It amazed him how happy he felt just being near her, but he wanted so much more.

He pulled the phone out of the clip on his waist-band. Flipping it open, he said, "Talk to me."

"I hope I didn't catch you at a bad time." Carter's voice sounded young, fresh and eager.

"You have no idea. What do you have for me?"

"I checked with the doctor at the camp and with InterAir Express, the shipping company on this end. Your missing drugs never made it into the country."

Rob walked to the large window at the back of the room. He suddenly had a very bad feeling in his bones. "Are you sure? It wouldn't be the first time officials in that neck of the woods skimmed supplies for the black market."

"I thought of that, too, but the invoice and papers are all in order. If the rest of the drugs left Austin, they didn't come here."

"It doesn't make sense. I know the woman who arranged the donations."

The silence on the other end of the line spoke volumes. After drawing a deep breath and blowing it out through pursed lips, Rob said, "You don't need to say it. I knew the guys at Memdelholm, too, but this isn't like that."

"If you say so." Carter's doubt was plain.

Rob didn't want to hear it. Didn't want to think it.

"Thanks for your help with this, Carter. I'll see what I can find out from this end. Any information over there about Whitney Harpswell?"

"Not yet, but I met with the coffee merchant you sent me to. He's agreed to take me to meet some of his—associates in the region. Thanks for getting the old guy to talk to me. He's a gold mine of information."

"Don't believe half of what he tells you. I mean it, Carter, be careful."

"For what it's worth, I know you wanted this assignment and I'm almost, but not quite, sorry I got it instead."

"Don't forget you're on *temporary* assignment there."

"Not if I can help it." Carter hung up and Rob closed his phone.

Raking a hand through his hair, Rob began pacing the small room. Only a portion of the drugs Nora had obtained in the name of her charity had reached their destination. Where were the rest?

He didn't like where this train of thought was leading him. Why would Nora siphon medical supplies away from Children of the Day? Why would anyone?

For money. The obvious answer made him sick to his stomach. He didn't want to admit that it might be true. His first instinct was to find Nora and ask her if she knew what had happened, but a growing uncertainty held him back.

He knew the hospital had stopped financing the state-of-the-art unit she wanted so desperately. Where had the money come from that she donated to get construction started again? Could her determination to build the best pediatric cardiac unit in the southwest have prompted her to get the money by illegal means?

No. It wasn't possible. He couldn't be in love with someone capable of doing such a thing.

I've only known her a couple weeks. How can I be so sure? Please, God, help me. I don't know what to think.

He hated the doubts piling up in his brain, but he couldn't stop them. He had been duped before.

Men he called friends, men he had fought beside and bled with had made a fool of him—for money. His respect and admiration for them had blinded him to the truth.

He glanced at his watch. Before he confronted anyone or revealed what he had leaned, he had some serious investigating to do. This time, he wouldn't allow his personal feelings to keep him from getting to the bottom of what was really going on.

After leaving the pediatric floor, he took the elevator to the third level. He walked down the hallway and entered Nora's office. To his relief, Carmen sat behind the receptionist's desk. She looked up and gave him a wide smile. With one hand she patted her dark hair into place.

"Mr. Dale, how nice to see you again. I thought you were going to be in surgery with Dr. Blake."

"I'm on my way there in a couple of minutes. There are a few facts I wanted to check out first. Maybe you can help me so I don't have to bother Nora."

"Sure. What do you need?"

He tried to sound nonchalant as he parked his hip on the corner of the desk, but his heart was racing. "I know Nora sometimes receives medical supplies for Children of the Day. Do they come through this office or through her home?"

"Through the hospital. Children of the Day has a large storage area here. It wouldn't be possible to keep such a volume of materials at her home. Besides, there are federal regulations regarding handling of medical supplies that are very strict. Children of the Day receives thousands of pounds of supplies from hundreds of different companies and organizations each year."

"It must be difficult to keep track of it all. Do hospital employees have access to the area?" He wanted his investigation to lead him away from Nora's involvement.

"We keep the keys here in the office. If I'm working and things come in for Children of the Day, Delia has very specific instructions for me to follow. All the paperwork is handled by her or by Dr. Blake."

"What about Dr. Kent?"

"He sometimes oversees donation arrivals when Dr. Blake is busy, but he uses our key. What is this about?"

He didn't want to lie so he settled on a half truth. "I'm just looking for a little more background information in case I need filler for a piece. Do you know which shipping company Nora uses when she sends donated supplies and drugs overseas?"

"She uses InterAir Express." It was the company Carter had mentioned.

He needed to know who had arranged that shipment. "Are they a reliable carrier?"

"I've never heard any complaints, but I can tell you that if Delia thought they weren't doing their job, she'd go elsewhere."

"Is there a way to see when the last two or three shipments were sent and when they arrived? That would give me an idea of how reliable and prompt they are."

Carmen clicked through to the company's Web site and logged on. "It looks like it took five days to get five cases of antibiotics to the Middle East, but it only took two days to get twenty cases of antibiotics to the Dominican Republic."

Quickly Rob jotted down the name of the clinic where the drugs had been delivered in the Caribbean. He said, "You can't beat that for good service. How is it all paid for?"

"Children of the Day has a corporate account and so does Dr. Blake, but I'm not sure I should be looking this kind of stuff up for you."

"I'm sorry. I get carried away sometime. You've been a big help, Carmen. Could you do one final little favor for me?"

She bit her lip. "That depends."

He reached out, lifted her hand from the computer mouse and planted a kiss on her knuckles as he gave her his best hangdog look. "I'm late for Ali's surgery. Could I borrow another set of scrubs from Dr. Kent?"

She blushed as she slowly drew her hand away. "Of course. I'll get them for you." She rose from her chair and went into the next room.

Leaning down, Rob grabbed the mouse and clicked through several more shipping files. His heart sank when he saw a dozen recent shipments to Mexico and the Dominican Republic had been charged to Nora's account and not to

Children of the Day. Everything kept pointing back to Nora's involvement. There had to be something he was missing.

Why had she sent the drugs somewhere other than the refugee camp in the Middle East? There had to be a simple explanation. Maybe the charity had a branch operating in the Caribbean that he didn't know about. Perhaps the need was simply greater there and Nora had responded by dividing the shipment.

He heard the door to Dr. Kent's office open. Clicking the files closed, he rose and took the uniform from Carmen. "Thanks, sweetie, you've been a great help."

Carmen smiled at him. "Little Ali will be in my prayers this afternoon."

"Mine, too. I'd better get going. I'll see you later. Be sure and tell Harold I think he's a blessed man to have a wife like you."

She waved his compliment aside. "Honey, I tell my husband that every day."

Rob grinned and said goodbye, but outside the office his smile faded. He took the elevator to the fifth floor and made his way to the surgical waiting room. It was nearly full. Seeing Anna and Olga across the room, he crossed to where they were sitting and dropped into an empty chair beside them.

"Have they brought Ali by yet?" he asked.

"Just a few minutes ago."

Glancing around, Rob noticed Marlon's absence. "Where's General Willis?"

"He and Pastor Fields have gone to the chapel."

"That's good. I'd better get going or I'll miss the surgery." He rose, but paused, then asked, "Anna, does Children of the Day have an operation in the Caribbean?"

"Not at present, although we've talked about starting one in Haiti. Why?"

He didn't want to upset her until he knew more. "I'm just trying to get a better sense of how widespread your organization is."

She smiled sadly. "I wish we could do more."

"You're doing great work," he assured her. "God will bless your efforts."

Olga covered Anna's hand with her own. "I believe that He will. Look after little Ali in there for us, Rob. We'll be out here praying that He blesses Dr. Blake's efforts. She has our little boy's life in her hands."

Rob nodded. Nora might have all the answers to the questions racing through his mind, but he couldn't ask her about it now. She needed her full concentration on the delicate surgery she was about to perform.

Rob left the waiting room but paused outside

the surgical suite doors. Pulling his cell phone out, he placed a call to Encore Investigations. He got the usual recording. When it was done playing, he said, "Murray, this is Rob Dale. I need you to check into a clinic in the Dominican Republic. I'm going to be out of touch for the next four hours, so leave me a message if you find out anything."

Rob recited the name and address from the shipping company records and then hung up and turned off his phone. Somehow, he was going to have to stand beside Nora for the next several hours and not ask her what she knew about the missing drugs. He prayed for patience.

Nora scrubbed in, donned her operating garb and backed through the operating room door with her wet arms curled in front of her. The electric cord for her electronic magnifying loops hung down her back from the headpiece like a long tail. One of the nurses came forward with a sterile towel, and Nora used it to dry her hands.

Ali was already asleep on the table. His eyes were taped shut and a white tube protruded from his mouth. At the head of the table the anesthesiologist had already connected the boy to a ventilator. An array of machines stood close by, and Nora looked to the perfusion technologist who would be managing the heart–lung bypass machine. "Are you ready?"

"We're good to go, Doctor."

Nora looked around the room. Rob hadn't yet arrived.

Dr. Kent came in behind her and accepted a towel from the same nurse. "This is going to be short and sweet, right? I've got a golf game scheduled this afternoon."

"That's my plan, Peter. It should be a straightforward repair."

The door to the scrub room opened again, and Nora relaxed as Rob came in.

Turning to one of the nurses, Nora said, "Would you please place a footstool behind me after I'm in position so that Mr. Dale can view the procedure, then we can get started."

Nora stepped up to the table. When Rob was in position behind her, she looked over her shoulder. "Can you see all right?"

"I'm fine," he answered quietly. His voiced seemed strained, but perhaps it was only the surgical mask making it sound distorted.

She turned back to the patient. Playing out the steps of the procedure in her mind, a calmness settled over her. Rob's solid presence behind her gave her an odd sense of comfort. She had wondered if he would prove to be a distraction, but it seemed that he had just the opposite effect.

She held out her hand and said, "Scalpel."

Twenty minutes into the operation, Nora realized Ali's surgery was going to be anything but routine. One problem after another cropped up. His blood pressure dropped without warning, prompting adjustments in the anesthetic being use. After that, she found unexpected scar tissue over the front of his heart. A result, no doubt, of the force of the blast that had torn the inside of his heart. It was something she hadn't anticipated and it slowed the pace of the operation while she gingerly worked her way through it.

When it came time to cool his body and stop his heart, the perfusion technologist announced there was trouble with the heart–lung bypass machine. It wasn't cooling the blood circulating through Ali's small body properly.

While the tech and another nurse worked to discover what was wrong, Rob spoke quietly behind Nora. "What does that mean?"

"It means I have to use another method to stop his heart."

"Like what?"

"I'll use iced sterile saline and pour it over the heart to stop it instead. It is just as effective, but I'll have to be much quicker." It was another problem that plagued what should have been a simple repair.

With Ali's small heart open at last, Nora studied the jagged tear in the thick membrane between the ventricles of his heart. "What do you think, Peter? Would it be better to trim tissue and make a neat hole I can close with a Dacron patch or spend additional time stitching this up?"

When he didn't answer, she glanced up at him. "Peter?"

He blinked. "Sorry. I was a thousand miles away for a second."

"Were you in Cancun again, Dr. Kent?" one of the nurses joked.

"Santo Domingo...or I will be in two days, thank goodness. What's the problem, Nora?"

She indicated where she was working. "Would you trim and patch this hole or stitch it?"

He bent his head to peer through his loupes. "I say trim and patch."

She nodded in agreement and set to work.

"We're cooling now," the perfusionist announced.

Nora relaxed. "That's good to hear. Now I won't have to rush."

Twenty minutes later she had a neat patch in

place and was satisfied that it would restore Ali's heart to normal function. She looked at the perfusionist. "Can we warm him now?"

"Yes, all the systems are working."

"Good. Warm our little boy."

Nora watched the heart, waiting for the first sign that it would begin beating on its own. Minutes passed.

"We're there," the perfusion technologist announced.

Nora frowned. "I don't have any activity. Are you sure he is warm enough?"

"Yes," the perfusionist was frowning over his machine.

"Better shock him," Dr. Kent suggested.

Nora looked at the closest nurse. "Give me the paddles."

The nurse handed her the internal defibrillator paddles, two foot-long wands with silver-dollar-sized discs on the ends. Nora gave the nurse the settings she wanted and then called out, "Clear."

She checked to make sure no one was touching Ali's body or the table he lay on, then she placed the paddles on either side of his heart and hit the button. The current made his heart jump, but it didn't keep going.

"What's the matter?" Rob asked.

Nora had almost forgotten he was there, but the sound of his voice steadied her. "His heart is proving to be a little stubborn. It doesn't want to restart."

After calling out a higher setting, Nora positioned the paddles again and delivered a bigger shock. Still nothing.

Fear settled in the pit of her stomach. Putting the paddles aside, she placed her hand around Ali's heart and began compressing it.

"Come on," she bit out through tight lips. "Don't do this. Don't die on me."

Chapter Fourteen

Nora stopped massaging Ali's heart and called for drugs that would help. When they had been given, she picked up the paddles and shocked him again. Still nothing. Beneath her mask, she could taste blood where she had bitten her lips.

"What do you want to do?" Dr. Kent asked.

"He's okay for a while longer on the heart–lung machine, but you know as well as I do we can't keep him on it forever. This shouldn't be happening."

"Don't give up on him." She heard the pleading in Rob's voice, and it doubled the pain she was already feeling.

"Give him another dose of epi." She started massaging the heart again. Another round of shocks followed.

"Come on. Come on." As the minutes ticked

by, her hand began to ache. A nurse called out the time and Nora's heart sank.

Suddenly, she felt a Rob place his hand gently in the center of her back. Softly, he said, "The Lord is my shepherd, I shall not want. He maketh me to lie down in green pastures: He leadeth me beside the still waters."

"He restoreth my soul," she continued with reverence. She knew the passage from her childhood. Deep in her heart, she felt God's presence as a vital living thing within. Ali's life was in God's hands. Her life was in God's hands. Her baby daughter was safe and loved with Him in Heaven. She could let go of her grief and pain.

Tears filled her eyes and she swallowed hard, then whispered, "I'm not giving up on you, Ali. God, help me to save this child."

With his hand on Nora's shoulders, Rob could feel the renewed strength fill her body. She called out for more drugs and then lifted the paddles and placed them on Ali's heart again. "Clear!"

Rob heard a tiny blip and glanced at the monitor. There it was again. He sucked in a deep breath as the wavy line became a strong, even beat. Collective sighs of relief echoed around the room, and Rob felt weak in the knees.

"Okay, let's get our boy closed up and out of here," Nora said. She started back to work, but Rob heard the clear relief in her voice.

"I can close," Dr. Kent said.

Nora shook her head. "No, this is one case I want to finish myself."

Thirty minutes later, Rob watched as Ali, still asleep, was wheeled out of the operating room. Nora pulled off her mask and her bulky surgical gown. She looked ready to drop, but there was an air of peace about her as she smiled up at him. "I need to talk to Ali's grandfather and make sure Ali is settled in PICU, then I'd like to buy you a cup of coffee. What do you say?"

"That sounds good. I'll come with you."

Once outside the OR, Rob followed Nora to the waiting room. Marlon rose to his feet when he saw her. "How is he?"

"He's fine now." Nora smiled. "He's fine," she called out loudly so that everyone in the room could hear.

"Thank the Lord," Marlon said, and sat down abruptly. A cheerful buzz broke out as people patted each other on the back and hugged one another.

Nora sat down beside Marlon. "It was touch and go for a while. He may need to spend a little longer in the hospital than I originally said. You can go up and see him in another thirty minutes."

He took her hand and shook it. "Thank you, Dr. Blake."

"You're welcome, sir."

Rising she looked at Rob. He saw such happiness in her eyes that it stole his breath.

As they rode up to the next floor on the elevator with a half dozen other people, Nora reached over to take his hand. Leaning toward him, she whispered, "Thanks."

"For what?"

She smiled softly at him. "For being there today."

The elevator doors opened and they stepped off together. Even after she let go of his hand, the warmth of her touch remained. When they reached the PICU, she stopped at the desk while Rob continued into Ali's room.

There were several nurses at the bedside, checking IV fluids and giving medications. Ali was still asleep. He looked so small in the bed. His thick, black eyelashes lay like dark crescents against his pale cheeks. Rob stepped up and laid a hand on the boy's head and whispered a prayer for his recovery. He knew that Ali wasn't out of the woods, but he felt in his heart that the Lord had great plans for the little man.

Nora came in with the head nurse at her side. As the two of them continued to confer, Rob stepped out of the room and turned on his cell phone. He had two messages. They were both from Encore Investigation. Rob hit Okay to play the first one.

"Rob, Murray here. I couldn't find anything on the clinic you gave me so I checked with my contacts at Interpol. The clinic is bogus. The place is a front for black market drugs throughout the islands. The local authorities moved in on it an hour ago but the place was empty. These guys never stay at one location for long. Whoever shipped your drugs had to know exactly where and when to send them. It was no accident."

Rob leaned against the nearest wall and balled his free hand into a fist. Someone involved with Children of the Day had deliberately misdirected desperately needed medication into illegal hands. It couldn't have been Nora. She wouldn't do that.

He walked to the doorway and looked in. She was listening to Ali's chest with a stethoscope and peering intently at the monitor over his bed.

Rob turned away and opened his phone to listen to the next message. Maybe Murray had found out the shipment had been a mistake.

"Hey, Dale, I almost forgot. I uncovered why you might have heard the name Hannor Pharmaceuticals. The World Health Organization was investigating Bernard Blake before his death. There were accusations his company re-labeled outdated measles vaccines then donated tons of it to poor villages throughout Indonesia. U.S. tax breaks on donated drugs are equal to their fair market value. The money kept his company going long enough to recover and prosper in the next few years.

"No one would have been the wiser except that there was an outbreak of measles in Indonesia a year later. A lot of kids died who had been vaccinated. After Blake's death, his wife broke up the company and sold it off, so the investigation was dropped. That's all I've got for you."

At the end of the message, Rob snapped his phone shut. Pressing his fingers to his temple, he struggled to hold on to his self-control. He wanted to drag Nora out of Ali's room and demand answers. No wonder she had evaded his questions about her husband and his business. He paced the hall until she appeared, a welcoming smile on her face.

"Are you ready for that coffee?" she asked.

"Nora, I need to talk you. We've got a problem."

Her smile faded. "You look so serious. What wrong?"

He stepped closer. "Three thousand vials of antibiotics were shipped from your office to black market drug dealers in the Caribbean instead of to the refugee camp in the Middle East. What do you know about it?"

Nora stared at Rob in complete shock. She couldn't believe her ears. "I don't know anything about it. Are you sure?"

"My source is positive."

"How could such a thing happen?"

His eyes never left hers. "Nora, the shipping invoice has your signature on it. It was paid for with your credit card."

A sick sensation settled in her stomach. "Rob, are you accusing me of stealing the medicine?"

His silence hurt like a physical blow. She said, "I didn't do it."

"I want to believe you."

"Then why don't you?" she snapped.

He stepped closer until he was looming over her. Softly, he said, "I've had the feeling since we met that you are hiding something from me. What is it, Nora?"

Unable to meet his gaze, she looked down.

"I'm sorry. There are other people I have to consider."

"Now is the time for the truth."

"You really think I'm involved in this, don't you?" Tears pricked her eyes, but she had spent years putting her emotions on hold while she did her job. She called up that willpower now and crossed her arms over her chest.

"I want to believe you, Nora, but how can I when you won't be honest with me. I know about the outdated measles vaccines."

Her heart dropped like a stone as her worst fear materialized. Pamela would be devastated. Nora couldn't protect her anymore.

She glared at Rob. "So you've been investigating me from the start. Was your story about Children of the Day and Ali's surgery just a ruse to get close to me?" Shaking her head, she answered before he could. "Of course it was. All of this—us—it was nothing but a means to an end."

"That's not true. My assignment was Children of the Day and Ali. I admit I had someone look into your background, but that was before we became involved."

Her mind was spinning, making it hard to focus. "What a fool I've been."

"Nora, a lot of people are going to start

asking for an explanation when this story gets out."

"You mean when *your* story hits the press."

Spinning on her heel, she marched down the hallway unable to see for the tears that burned her eyes. She had been about to tell Rob that she was falling in love with him. How could she have been so mistaken? He didn't love her. He had only used her.

She didn't wait for the elevator, but took the stairs down to the third floor. Rob followed close behind her.

Nora yanked open her office door and stormed inside as she worked to get a grip on her emotions.

Carmen looked up, her eyes wide. She quickly closed the e-mail missive on her computer. "Dr. Blake, you startled me. Is something wrong? Did the surgery go okay?"

"Ali Willis should make a full recovery."

"That's good. Well, if you don't need me, I was just getting ready to leave."

Nora heard the door behind her open but she didn't turn around. She knew who was there.

"You may go home, but before you do, will you get me the files for the all of the medical shipments I've made for Children of the Day for the past year?"

Carmen looked from Rob back to Nora. "Certainly, but can I ask why?"

"Because Mr. Dale thinks I'm a thief." Her throat closed around the words and she couldn't speak.

Rob said, "Part of the last antibiotic shipment has gone astray and we want to find out how that happened."

Carmen glared at him. "Is this why you were asking questions earlier?"

"I had a suspicion and I wanted to check it out before I said anything."

"You used me to pry into Dr. Blake's private business. Dr. Blake, I am so sorry." Carmen's anger boiled over. "Do you want me to call security and have this jerk thrown out of the hospital?"

Nora raised her chin. She wouldn't cry even if her heart was breaking. "Yes. That is exactly what I want you to do."

The next afternoon, Rob sat at the small table in his motel room and stared at his blank computer screen with a sick feeling that he was sure would never go away. He had a story now that would wow his boss. It was the kind of story most reporters dreamed of uncovering… but he couldn't find the words to tell it. He forced himself to type the headline that would ensure his promotion back to the Middle East.

Prominent Pediatric Heart Surgeon Uses Charity to Cover Black Market Drug Deals.

Holding down the delete key, he watched the words disappear letter by letter from his screen. If only there was some way to make them disappear from his mind.

"Lord, why did You bring me here? Why let me fall in love with this woman? What lesson am I supposed to learn? Please, I don't know what I'm supposed to do."

The only answer that kept coming to mind was that he should believe Nora. He loved her. He knew in his heart that she couldn't have done this—but he had been fooled before.

A knock at the door forced him to get up. He expected it to be housekeeping making their daily rounds, but when he pulled open the door he saw Pamela Blake standing in front of him looking angry and determined.

"Pamela, what are you doing here?" Rob glanced behind him at the laptop lying on the table.

"I was coming here to punch your lights out, but my cooler side has prevailed." She fisted her hands on her hips. "Nora didn't do this, and I can't prove it by myself. Rob, I need your help."

He sighed. "I don't want to believe it myself, but everything points to her involvement."

Pamela took a step closer. "Then someone is making it look that way."

He turned aside. "I know that you love her."

"At least consider the possibility that she didn't do it," Pamela insisted, following him into the room.

He sat down at the small table and closed his laptop. He hadn't slept, couldn't eat, couldn't think of anything but the look of pain on Nora's face. "I want to believe that she is innocent."

Pamela sank to her knees beside him and gripped his arm. "Then *believe* her. Listen to your heart."

"A heart can be fooled—and broken."

"That's your excuse for not helping her? Your heart is broken? Get over it. So what if she kept a painful part of her past a secret? It's her life. Now that life is about to be destroyed."

He raked a hand through his hair. "I used to think I was a good judge of character, but I found out just how wrong I could be. I have to look at the evidence now."

She shook him. "This isn't about you, Rob.

This isn't about how wrong you've been in the past. This is about Nora's reputation. It's about her future. I thought you cared about her."

"I do."

"Then why are you sitting here feeling sorry for yourself instead of getting out there and *proving* she didn't do anything wrong."

He stared into Pamela's angry eyes and saw the truth in what she was saying. He *had* been feeling sorry for himself. He'd been wallowing in self-pity. The only thing making a fool out of him this time was his own doubt and insecurity.

The reason he couldn't write the story was because he didn't believe it.

So he had been wrong about his friends Benny and Drake. He wasn't responsible for the bad choices they made. It didn't mean he had to give up trusting people. Perhaps that was what God wanted him to discover.

He forced his tired brain into action. "Who could do it?"

"I don't know. That's why I came to you."

"Okay, who could physically do it? Who has access to her files, the storage, shipping information, her credit card?"

"Does that mean you'll help her?"

"Yes. Where is she?" He grabbed his car keys and started out of the room.

"At home, crying her eyes out and telling me that everything is fine. She always tells me everything is fine."

Rob stopped and looked at Pamela. He saw a young woman in charge of her own life, and he had to admire her. Nora was blessed to have Pamela as a friend and as a daughter.

"Pamela, if this gets out, you are going to hear some things that will be hard to accept."

"You're talking about my father."

"Yes."

"I know that he was being investigated if that's what you mean. I also know that he made a terrible mistake when the company was in financial trouble and he tried very hard to make up for it later. His decision haunted him."

"Did Nora know about it?"

"Not until the investigation started. When she found out, they had a terrible fight and Dad left. I may have lost my father in that skiing accident, but Nora lost her husband and then her newborn baby all in the same week. I let her think she was protecting me by keeping the information and the press away from me because she *needed* to do that."

"You're a remarkable woman."

She smiled. "I know a great guy who thinks the same thing. His name is Gary. You should meet him."

"I'd like that."

Rob followed Pamela back to her house and parked his truck behind her car. She hurried up the front steps and opened the door, but he hesitated. How could Nora ever forgive him for doubting her?

Pamela looked at him. "What?"

"I don't know what to say to her."

"*I'm sorry* is a good start. If you want to add that you've been a complete jerk, that's entirely up to you. She's downstairs. Watch out for the dog. He gets cranky when she gets upset."

"Thanks for the warning."

Rob walked down the steps to Nora's workshop with his heart pounding harder than it did when he finished a ten-mile run. He didn't have a chance to plan what he would say because Conan suddenly appeared at the bottom step with his teeth bared. He growled with convincing menace.

Nora came to stand behind the dog. She had pretty much the same expression in her eyes. "What are you doing here?"

* * *

Nora couldn't believe that Rob had the nerve to show his face in her own home. "Have you come to smear more mud on me?"

"I came to offer my help."

"You've helped enough. You've got your story. Now, get out."

Conan growled louder. Rob slowly sank to his haunches and extended his hand to the dog. "Nora, I'm sorry. I'm a complete idiot. You are brave and caring woman, and I know you didn't do this. I doubted you because I had lost faith in myself, in my ability to believe wholeheartedly in others. You're innocent and I want to help you prove it."

Nora wanted so badly to believe him. She took a step closer and laid her hand on Conan's head. "How?"

Conan stopped growling and sat. Rob rose to his feet. "I need to get back into your office."

"Why?"

"Because my gut tells me that's where the answers are."

"Why should I trust you now?" Her voice cracked and she bit her upper lip.

"Trust me because I'm a good reporter."

"Ha!"

"Look, I know I made a big mistake. I'm

asking you to forgive me. I don't blame you if you can't. I will never doubt you again as long as we live. I love you, Nora. I don't deserve you, but I can't help loving you. Maybe we've only known each other for a couple weeks, but God put you right in front of me for a reason."

There was no doubting the sincerity of his words. His eyes pleaded for her understanding more eloquently than his words. He took another step closer, holding out his hand to her.

She sniffed once. "You really hurt me."

"I know I did. I can't begin to tell you how sorry I am."

"I thought you were a good man."

He descended another step. "I need to keep working on that. I could use your help."

"I thought my husband was a good man, too but he…he chose money over…over the lives of children."

Rob reached the bottom step and pushed Conan out of the way with his knee. "I know what he did, but I'm not him. You and I can make a fresh start, together."

He wrapped his arms around her. She leaned into him, letting go of her last burden. "I love you, too, Rob. You have no idea how much."

"I love you enough to let your dog chew my shoes while I'm wearing them."

She laughed through her tears as she looked down at Conan and back up at Rob. "You and Conan are going to have to work that out between you."

"We'll come to an understanding. Now, let's go to your office and see if we can figure out who wants to frame you."

Chapter Fifteen

Rob sat at the computer in Nora's outer office and stared at the screen, determined to find the answers he was looking for. "Let's start with who could do this. Who has access to everything regarding medical supplies for Children of the Day?"

"Myself."

"Honey, I think we've ruled you out."

"Okay, someone in housekeeping or security? They have keys to everything at the hospital."

"But how would they get access to the shipping account? It's password protected."

"Anna Terenkov can get into the account, as can Delia and Carmen."

"Didn't you notice the unusual charges on your statements?"

"The money comes out of a special bank

account. My financial adviser handles everything to do with those specific funds. As long as the money was being used for Children of the Day, he wouldn't question the withdrawals. I only used part of the money for myself once."

"Why is that?"

"It's from my husband's life insurance. I swore I would only use it to make a difference for children. I was trying to make amends for what he did. I wanted to make sure the money was going for something worthwhile, something that would last."

"That's where the donation for the PICU construction came from."

"Yes. That is the one selfish thing I've done with the money."

"Building a state-of-the-art medical facility for children is hardly selfish. Who knows about the account?"

"Anna and my accountant. That's it."

Rob highlighted the screen and hit Print. "Okay, let's take a look at the dates of all the shipments over the past year and see if we can discover which ones didn't go where they belonged."

"These." Nora pointed out seven shipments. "Nothing should have gone to Mexico or to the Caribbean."

"Good. Now, do you have Carmen and Delia's work schedules?"

"I think so. Delia does the payroll." Nora moved to the filling cabinet and after a few minutes of searching pulled out a folder.

Rob took it from her and began to compare the dates. After double-checking them, he heaved a sigh. "I don't see a pattern. Delia was here most of these dates, but not for the last two shipments. Unless she and Carmen are in it together, I think we can rule them out."

Nora tilted her head to the side. "Let me see those shipment dates again."

Rob handed her the paper. "What is it? Do you see something?"

"Yes. And if I'm right, we need to hurry. Come on." She turned and left the office. Rob raced to keep up with her.

Once they reached the parking lot, Rob unlocked the door of his truck and Nora slid into the passenger's seat. After hurrying around to the driver's side, he got in and said, "Are you going to share what you know or keep me guessing?"

"I'm hoping that I'm wrong." She gave him directions, and a few minutes later they pulled up in front of a high-rise apartment complex a few blocks from the hospital.

Inside the building, they took the elevator to the twelfth floor. Rob followed her as she walked down the hallway to Apartment 1209 and knocked.

After a few seconds, the door opened. Peter Kent looked at them in surprise. At his feet were two large suitcases. "Nora, what are you doing here?"

"We have a problem at the office, Peter."

"Can't it wait until I get back from my weekend off?"

"Where are you going?" Rob asked.

"Santo Domingo."

Rob crossed his arms over his chest. "That's in the Dominican Republic, isn't it?"

"Yes, and I need to get to the airport."

Nora carefully watched her partner's face as she said, "Mr. Dale has discovered that someone has been stealing medical supplies from Children of the Day."

Peter frowned. "No kidding?"

"Yes," Rob added. "And that someone has been trying to make it look like Dr. Blake was responsible."

"That's terrible. Who at Children of the Day would do such a thing?"

"According to these shipping invoices, it's someone at Mercy Medical Center."

Peter shoved his hands in his pockets. "What shipping invoices?"

She held out the papers. "Each one of these shipments was made on days that I worked at Fort Bonnell."

"That's interesting, but I don't see what it has to do with me. I have a cab waiting downstairs and I need to get going or I'll miss my flight."

"The other odd thing about these dates," Nora continued, "is that each one of them happens to be exactly one week before your minivacations this year. You've been to Mexico and to the Caribbean a total of seven times in the last twelve months."

Peter took a step backward. "That doesn't mean anything. I like the beach scene."

Rob stepped forward and pulled his cell phone from his pocket. "I imagine a check of your credit card receipts will show that you visited the same locations where these supplies went on every occasion. What better way to make sure you get your money than to go in person?"

Nora closed her eyes. "Peter, how could you?"

He dashed toward the door, but Rob blocked his way and easily overpowered him by locking one of Peter's arms behind his back. "You're not going anywhere. Nora, call 911."

"Nora, please," Peter pleaded. "We can work this out."

"Tell me why you did it," she demanded.

"My ex-wife is still getting half of everything I make because of our stupid prenuptial agreement. I needed money that she couldn't get her hands on. The drugs and supplies are all still going to poor people."

"Made poorer by the prices they are forced to pay on the black market while you get richer on the side," Rob hissed. "How did you get access to Children of the Day's account information?"

"I saw Delia giving instructions to Carmen in the office when she was first hired. Carmen wrote them down. She keeps them in a notebook in the bottom drawer of her desk. I made a copy one day when she went out to lunch. After the first time it was easy and you never caught on."

"Oh, but we did catch on. Thanks to Rob. I never thought you would stoop so low, Peter." Nora gave him a look of disgust, then pulled her cell phone from her purse and dialed the police.

A few days later, Rob walked out of his motel room and pulled the door shut. He paused with his hand on the knob. He was closing the door on an important chapter in his life. One that had changed him forever.

He glanced over his shoulder. It was still dark out, but the first faint light could be seen touching the hills and buttes to the east. He smiled as he headed for the stairs at the side of the building. A new day was dawning. A new chapter of his life was just starting.

He carried his suitcase down the wide steps at the end of the wing. As he approached his ride, he extended his electronic key and pressed the button, and the rear hatch opened. He threw his suitcase in, slammed the hatch and walked toward the driver's side door. He had a hand on the handle and was about to open the door when he saw her standing a few feet away.

She looked so beautiful that it took his breath away. She took a step toward him. "I know you're leaving today."

"I was on my way to see you first." He walked toward her and held out his arms. She flew into his embrace, and he relished the feel of her safe in his arms. Was there any man in the world who was more blessed?

"I miss you already," she whispered.

He drew away to cup her face between his hands and gaze into her eyes. "I'll be back as soon as I can get things settled in Washington."

"I can't believe you're really moving here. We don't have much armed conflict in Prairie Springs. You might be bored out of your skull."

"You will never bore me."

"You can go on overseas assignments if that's what you want. You know I would never stand in your way."

"I know that. I also know that all I care about is right in front of me. I don't need anything else. Besides, Fort Bonnell is the largest military base in the United States. I think a good investigative reporter like myself can dig up a few stories for the Midwest bureau of *Liberty and Justice*. If not, I can always freelance for the Austin papers."

"I hope this is what you really want."

"I want to be where you are. You make me happy."

"Oh, Rob. You've given me so much. You brought God back into my life, and you've shown me that forgiveness is so much better than bitterness. You make me happy, too." She threw her arms around him.

"I'm glad," he whispered against her neck.

Drawing back, she brushed the tears from her face. "You still have to stop by the hospital and see Ali. He was moved out of the PICU last evening."

"That's great news."

"And you need to stop by Children of the Day. Everyone wants to thank you for uncovering Dr. Kent's sad scheme."

"At least he is making restitution for his crimes. The money will go a long way in helping other children."

"We are all praying for him. He needs our forgiveness as much as anyone. Have you heard anything from your friend about Whitney Harpswell?"

"He called late last night. All he has come up with are dead ends. I'm going to stop by Evan's ranch and let him know before I leave town."

"Tell him not to give up hope."

"I will."

She tucked her hands in her jean jacket pockets. "So, have you had breakfast?"

"Not yet."

Nora grinned, happy and grateful to be able to spend a few hours in his company. God willing they would spend many more hours, days and years together, but she would never take her time with him for granted. She said, "I have a picnic basket with coffee and bread and jam. I know a place with a great view of the sunrise. Are you up for a hike?"

"With you? Always."

* * * * *

Don't miss the fifth
Homecoming Heroes *book,*
A TEXAS THANKSGIVING
by Margaret Daley.
Available November 2008
from Steeple Hill Love Inspired.

Dear Reader,

I hope you enjoyed my story, *A Matter of the Heart*. As a nurse myself, I have tremendous respect for surgeons who operate on children and for cardiac surgeons in particular. Their work is awe-inspiring and difficult beyond belief. I've taken many of my little patients into surgery over the years. Each time I have marveled at the doctors who worked with microscopic precision as Nora Blake did in this story.

As marvelous as a surgeon's skills may be, the recovery of these children would not be possible without nurses, respiratory therapists, the people who work in laboratories and X-ray departments, and countless others toiling behind the scenes in every hospital. Just as it takes a village to raise a child, so does it take a village to care for the sickest of our children. To health care workers and hospital employees everywhere, may God continue to bless each of you in the work you do for Him.

Patricia Davids

DISCUSSION QUESTIONS

1. What themes were emphasized through-out the book?

2. What message did you take away from this story?

3. Dr. Nora Blake believed in science, not faith, to heal her patients. Do you think this is typical of her profession? Why?

4. Rob Dale was determined to uncover "the truth" about Children of the Day and about Nora. Do you feel he was justified in digging into her past?

5. A frequent setting in this story was the hospital where Nora worked. Have you or someone close to you had a child who needed surgery? How did facing that crisis affect your faith or the faith of those you know?

6. Did the setting of the novel detract or add to your enjoyment of the story? Why?

7. What do you see as Rob's most "heroic" character trait? What was his least "heroic" trait?

8. If you could spend an hour with one character from this story, who would it be and what would you ask them?

9. The two main characters have very different professions and personalities in this story. Did you find it believable that they fell in love with each other? Why or why not?

10. Did the author portray Nora's spiritual growth in a way that felt believable? What things about her journey to God resonate with you?

11. Nora's deceased husband committed an unscrupulous act. Was she right or wrong in her determination to protect her stepdaughter from learning about it? Why?

12. Rob made the decision to give up a job he badly wanted to stay near Nora. Have you ever given up something important for another person? Was it ultimately a good decision?

13. Rob was put on the spot when he was asked about what would make the perfect date. What perfect date or dating disaster do you remember the most and why?

Love Inspired®
SUSPENSE
RIVETING INSPIRATIONAL ROMANCE

Watch for our new series of
edge-of-your-seat suspense novels.
These contemporary tales
of intrigue and romance
feature Christian characters
facing challenges to their faith...
and their lives!

Steeple
Hill®

Visit:
www.SteepleHill.com

Love Inspired. HISTORICAL

INSPIRATIONAL HISTORICAL ROMANCE

Engaging stories of romance,
adventure and faith,
these novels are set in
various historical periods
from biblical times
to World War II.

NOW AVAILABLE!

Steeple
Hill®